SECRET OF THE ORACLE

AN ANCIENT GREEK MYSTERY

D0928805

Look out for more *Ancient Greek Mysteries* by
Saviour Pirotta, published by Bloomsbury Education.

Mark of the Cyclops
Pirates of Poseidon (coming soon)

Visit www.bloomsbury.com/education
for more information.

SECRET OF THE ORACLE

AN ANCIENT GREEK MYSTERY

SAVIOUR PIROTTA

Illustrated by FREYA HARTAS

BLOOMSBURY EDUCATION
AN IMPRINT OF BLOOMSBURY
LONDON OXFORD NEW YORK NEW DELHI SYDNEY

Bloomsbury Education
An imprint of Bloomsbury Publishing Plc

50 Bedford Square
London
WC1B 3DP
UK

1385 Broadway
New York
NY 10018
USA

www.bloomsbury.com

First published in 2017

A catalogue record for this book is available from the British Library.

ISBN
PB: 978 1 4729 4016 2
ePub: 978 1 4729 4014 8
ePDF: 978 1 4729 4017 9

2 4 6 8 10 9 7 5 3 1

Typeset by Newgen Knowledge Works Pvt. Ltd., Chennai, India
Printed and bound in the UK by CPI Group (UK) Ltd, Croydon CR0 4YY

To find out more about our authors and books visit www.bloomsbury.com.
Here you will find extracts, author interviews, details of forthcoming
events and the option to sign up for our newsletters.

To Godwin Grech, a childhood friend
whose cork model of the Oracle at Delphi
inspired this story

CONTENTS

PROLOGUE

The Mother of Shadows

Winter, 433 BC

It was already dark when the girl with the unusually red hair crept out of the shed, peering this way and that. She was leaving the farm without her parents' permission and she didn't want to get caught. As she stole past the barn where her father slept, one of the family's goats bleated loudly. The girl froze in her tracks, her heart thumping. She did not start walking again

I

until she was sure her father was snoring. Then she made a dash for the gate.

Click!

The girl breathed a sigh of relief as she pulled the gate shut behind her. It didn't take her long to find the mountain path, and she hurried on without looking back. She needed to be quick if she was going to make it home before her parents woke up.

It was mid-winter and the air was sharp with the scent of pine. A sliver of new moon sat high in the sky above the mountain, glinting like the edge of a silver coin. It was surrounded by a multitude of stars, twinkling in the velvety darkness. The girl thought the new moon a good omen. She was named after the moon goddess and a new moon always brought her good luck.

There was snow on the ground and she was glad she'd put on her boots instead of her usual sandals. She was glad of the warm epiblema around her shoulders too. She had inherited the much-darned woollen shawl from her grandmother. Once a deep earthy brown, time had turned it to a muddy grey, but it was still a joy to wear. Whenever she snuggled into its prickly warmth, the girl got the feeling that the shade of her long-gone grandmother was close by, protecting her. It was a comforting feeling.

Her grandmother had once told the girl that the mountain was full of hidden magic created by the gods at the beginning of time. Its rocks and caves, streams and ravines were home to nymphs and muses. The ancient earth goddess slept unseen in the mountain still, her sleeping breath escaping through cracks in the rock to fill the air with a special power.

Sometimes the girl felt that she had inherited some of that power from her grandmother, who had been a well known seer.

Coming to a clear mountain spring, the girl stopped to drink. All around her the night breeze rustled the branches of the pine and laurel trees. Owls hooted in the darkness. From the corner of her eye, the girl caught sight of small amber lights flickering under the trees. Mountain wolves were watching her.

The girl was not scared of wolves. She believed them to be sacred creatures, messengers of the gods and protectors of the mountain.

She finished drinking and continued her walk upwards. Now she could make out the sound of voices coming down the stony path. The girl's hands immediately closed around an amulet hanging on a strip of leather around her neck.

It was too early in the year for mountain bandits, who could not use the high mountain pass while it was still blocked with snow and slippery with black ice. The voices must belong to goatherds. The girl slipped behind a pine tree and stood so still she seemed to become part of the tree. It was a trick she had learned a long time ago when hiding from bullies.

The girl with the red hair wasn't popular with the other children on the mountain. Her pale skin and green eyes marked her out as different, and a target for their pranks.

She waited until the chattering voices faded before stepping out of her hiding place.

After a while, the steep path levelled out and she came to a flat piece of ground. Before her stood the entrance to a cave, a dark wide-open mouth in the bony whiteness of the mountainside. There was a rocky altar in the middle of it, strewn with decaying offerings of fruit and vegetables. Beyond it, at the far end of the cave, the girl could see the glow of a burning fire.

She skirted past the altar and walked into the cave.

A dark outline behind the fire stirred. A whisper echoed in the girl's head.

'Is it you, my child? The girl with the fire-red hair?'

The girl approached. 'Yes, Mother of Shadows. It is me.'

The woman leaned forward and her shadow danced on the cave wall behind her. Bangles jingled as a stick-thin arm beckoned the girl closer. The wheezy voice spoke across the bonfire.

'I read it in the stones that you were coming to see me. Sit. It has been a long time since your last visit.'

The girl sat. 'My father only allows me to bring the goats up the mountain in summer. He says there is enough green grass for them in our fields during the winter. It's very difficult to get up here without anyone in the family noticing.'

The shadow nodded. 'But now there is something troubling you. You felt you had to take the risk and seek advice from your old teacher, your mentor.'

The girl pulled a small parcel from inside her peplos and placed it on the ground as an offering. 'Cheese from our farm, and preserved olives, picked by my sister last year,' she said. 'I keep having a vivid dream. The same one. I fear it is a warning of dangers to come.'

'You have tried to interpret your dream,' said the Mother of Shadows hoarsely. 'But the meaning eludes you. You hope that I can enlighten you, so you can evade the danger.'

The girl lowered her head, hiding her face.

'Tell me what you have seen, child,' said the Mother of Shadows gently, leaning closer to the fire so that her shadow grew bigger on the cave wall behind her.

'I go to sleep only to wake up and find I am not lying in my bed but on some sort of boat. It is leaking water and hurtling along a wild, dark river. The waves crash over my head, freezing me to the bone, and I cannot move. I seem to have lost the use of my legs and arms. There are shadows on the raft with me but I cannot work out if they are friends or foe. Chasing the raft is a third figure, its himation pulled up tight around its head, so that its face is obscured. Somehow I know it is a man.

'He is riding a turtle. Not a friendly turtle such as you might find at the seashore but a terrible monster with pointed teeth and fire-red eyes. It follows the raft at great speed, its jaws snapping wildly. Suddenly the wind blows the himation off the rider's head, revealing the face. It is a glowing skull with empty eyes.

'The rider is brandishing a spear and, as the monster turtle catches up with the raft, he lunges forward to throw it at me. Only a moment later, the raft goes over the edge of a precipice and I am plunged into a wet, roaring darkness. The shock of hitting the water always wakes me up and I find myself kicking out under my himation, a scream caught in my throat. That is what I see in my dream.'

The Mother of Shadows sat immobile for a long time, humming softly through closed lips. Now that she was leaning closer to the fire, the girl could see her face. The cheeks were lined and withered with age, the eyes just narrow slits under sooty eyebrows.

At last the old woman looked up from the flames. She reached to the floor and lifted a small clay cup, which she shook, one hand held over its mouth to stop the contents from spilling out.

'Pay attention, for tonight the goddess speaks through the colours. Choose a pebble.'

She held out the cup. The girl reached into it and held the pebble on the palm of her hand.

'Ah, the red one. The colour of fire and Python's blood.'

The Mother of Shadows' withered hand hovered over the red pebble, the fingers rippling, and then – suddenly – it froze.

'You are indeed in danger, my child,' gasped the old woman, grabbing the red pebble and holding it tight above the flames. 'Grave danger! The figure on the turtle seeks to destroy you, for you pose a great threat to it. You must protect yourself with charms and spells as I taught you. As for the two shadowy figures on the raft, do not be afraid of them. They are both child-men and they have nothing but goodness in their hearts. The goddess sends them to your rescue...'

CHAPTER ONE

An Important Decision

Two months later, early spring

'Can you believe it?' fumed Master Ariston as the front door crashed shut behind him. 'The idiot refused to pay me. He said the songs I sang at his party have made him the laughing stock of the city. The swindling, tight-fisted, gorgon-kissing son of a harpy! Has he never heard of comedy?'

He was about to kick a statue of the god Hermes when the door opened again and his precious lyre came flying out. It landed on the ground with a horrific twang as some of the strings snapped.

Master Ariston turned pale at the sound. 'How dare you?' he screeched as the door slammed shut once more. 'That lyre cost me the earth. I'll – I'll take you to court!'

Master Ariston is a well known poet and a songwriter. He travels around the Hellenic world performing his work at weddings and parties, which we call symposiums. I am Nico, his scribe. My job is to write down the hundreds of songs and poems that Master Ariston composes every year, sometimes right in the middle of a performance. A third person accompanies us. His name is Thrax and he is Master Ariston's personal slave. His duties include fetching the master's food, keeping his vast array of clothes in immaculate condition, tuning the lyre during performances and styling his curly beard. Master Ariston is very particular about his big bushy beard, which he insists on wearing in the latest fashion.

The man who had just refused to pay us was a powerful magistrate in Sicyon, a beautiful city known for its talented sculptors and award-winning charioteers. Sadly, Master Ariston did not praise either sculpture or chariot racing once in his songs, choosing instead to poke fun at Sicyon's ships, which are known to be inferior to Athenian vessels. The guests at the party had not seen the funny side of it and pelted us with overripe fruit and nuts.

Now we stood shivering in the morning cold outside the magistrate's front door, surrounded by huge wicker chests containing all our belongings. Thrax and I had started loading them on to Ariana, our donkey, while Master Ariston went to seek payment from our host.

We always lodge with the family Master Ariston is entertaining, and leave with a bag full of silver at the end of the festivities. But this time, the offended magistrate had refused to pay.

'What shall I do now? I am ruined,' wailed Master Ariston, ignoring the fact that the situation affected Thrax and me too. 'I didn't even have the chance to fetch my jewellery before the chief slave of the house showed me the door. It was hidden under my pillow.'

Thrax, who was used to our master's flair for drama, took command of the situation. 'Nico, you look after the master and our belongings. I'll get the jewellery.'

Thrax might be a slave, but he's is the sharpest thinker of us three. He's very strong and athletic too. Before we knew it, he had clambered up a grapevine and disappeared down inside the courtyard of the magistrate's house. We stood in silence, praying to Hermes he wouldn't get caught. Then the front door creaked open and Thrax slipped out with Master Ariston's precious jewellery wrapped in linen.

Master Ariston's sniffed with gratitude but he didn't thank Thrax. It's not that he mistreats slaves; he's just too self-absorbed to ever thank anyone.

'However did you manage that?' I asked.

Thrax grinned and shrugged, strapping an enormous wicker chest full of scrolls on to his back. Master Ariston insists on travelling with an entire library of classics for inspiration. 'It's easy to slip in and out of houses early in the morning. Everyone is so busy, no one gives you a second glance if you keep your head down and walk fast.'

Although I am not a slave myself, Thrax and I are best friends. We have formed a secret society that solves mysteries and tackles crime wherever we find it. It's called the Medusa League and so far it has four members: Thrax, myself, and two girls called Fotini and Gaia. They live in the city of Corinth where we solved our first mystery last year. All four of us wear special medallions with the face of the Medusa on them. It's our secret badge and I always have mine hanging round my neck.

Thrax and I were paid handsomely for solving our first mystery but I refused to take any of the reward. Thrax is trying to earn enough money to buy his freedom. His one dream is to be reunited with his mother in Thrace. All slaves dream of freeing themselves but the odds are heavily stacked against them. The cost is too high, the opportunities of earning money too few. The majority of slaves go to their grave without having tasted one moment of freedom in their wretched lives. I am determined it will be different for Thrax. He'll get his freedom and be able to have the fulfilling life everyone deserves.

I have my own dream. I want to be a famous writer whose stories are heard and admired all over the Hellenic world. For a long time I didn't know what kind of writing I wanted to do. But then Thrax suggested I write about the mysteries we solve. Not long poems with rhyming text, but stories with ordinary language that anyone can understand and enjoy. I have finished one already. It's called *The Mark of the Cyclops* and it's based on our first adventure in Corinth. I'm hoping I'll get the chance to give readings of it in symposiums when I'm a bit older.

Thrax looked up at the lightening sky. 'We need to get going if we are to make the boat back to Athens today, master.'

Master Ariston cleared his throat dramatically as Thrax helped him on to Ariana. 'I have come to a momentous decision, boys,' he announced. 'We are not going back home to Athens yet.'

Thrax and I looked at him in confusion. 'But we have booked our passage already, sir,' I said. 'Your father is expecting us. You are to sing at your cousin's son's naming ceremony in a few days.'

'My cousin's son will have to wait for his songs,' said Master Ariston haughtily. 'I hate disappointing the family but you will never succeed in this world if you go running home every time your father calls. You have to learn to say no when you need to.'

'So where are we going if not to Athens?' asked Thrax.

A broad grin spread across Master Ariston's face. 'Do you remember when we met Euripides, the acclaimed playwright, in Corinth?'

'Yes,' I replied. 'The meeting inspired you to start writing your own play.'

'I think I have what it takes to be a brilliant playwright,' said Master Ariston proudly. 'Perhaps the best in the world. One of the reasons my songs have lacked my trademark wit and sparkle lately is because I keep thinking about the stage instead of poetry. My attention is diverted.'

He sighed. 'But it's so risky to change careers at my age. I have climbed dizzying heights with my singing. My name is known and respected in households all over Hellas, even if the boorish magistrates of Sicyon fail to appreciate my brilliance. Should I risk it all by switching to writing plays full time? No matter how much I toss and turn in my bed at night, I can't make up my mind. I must seek the advice of the highest authority in the world and beyond. I must ask the mighty god of poetry, art and music himself. Boys, we are going to visit the famous oracle of Apollo at Delphi.'

CHAPTER TWO

The Mysterious Man
on the Beach

Delphi is a small but powerful city that sits on the lower slopes of Mount Parnassus, one of the highest mountains in Hellas. It is said that the mountain has been sacred since the beginning of time. It is a place of magic and mystery, where the gods speak to give mortals warnings and advice.

According to legend, Gaia, the earth goddess, once dwelt on Mount Parnassus, as did her son, the dragon Python. Apollo slew the dragon, making the mountain and the oracle his own. He lured priests from faraway Mycenae to become his servants at the temple. The city that grew up around it became known the world over. The rich and the poor, the powerful and the helpless all come flocking to the oracle for advice. No war in Hellas starts without generals consulting the oracle. No city is founded, no important journey undertaken before the Pythia, the priestess at the famous temple, speaks on behalf of the god.

The way from Sicyon to Delphi lies across a busy sea called the Gulf of Corinth. It is well known among sailors and travellers for its playful dolphins, and indeed a merry group of them followed our merchant ship as we sailed towards Kirrha, the port of Delphi.

We arrived there too late in the day to continue our journey but Thrax discovered some huts behind the docks where travellers could shelter for a very small fee. We settled Master Ariston in, fed and stabled Ariana, then set out to get some food from the local market.

'The man who sold us the bread said there was a fire in the woods outside the port,' I said to Thrax after we had given Master Ariston his dinner and found him a warm spot in the hut to sleep in. 'A lot of pine trees were destroyed. Let's go and find some burnt logs. I am running low on ink.'

I make my own ink by mixing finely ground soot with the sap of trees and a little water. It's an old skill I learned from an Egyptian scribe when still an apprentice. It makes a thick ink that sticks well to papyrus or parchment and does not fade easily with time.

'Good idea,' said Thrax. 'I could do with a walk.'

It was pitch dark by the time we set off, and we kept to the shoreline so we would not get lost. Away from the noisy port, the night was full of gentler sounds. I could hear owls hooting in the nearby pine trees, the cawing of seagulls overhead and the lapping of waves against the shore. They reminded me of Kos, the island where my parents live and work a small farm.

We passed hastily built altars set up to thank Apollo and Poseidon for safe journeys across the gulf. Then, coming to a bend in the road, we spotted a ghostly white shape hovering on the beach. A burning light floated lazily above it.

Thrax slowed his pace. 'What in the name of Zeus is that?'

'It could be the soul of a murdered pilgrim,' I said, only half joking. 'Or the ghost of a drowned sailor looking for the entrance to the underworld.'

Thrax narrowed his eyes to see better. 'It looks like a dancer to me. He has a flaming torch in his hand.'

He was right. A young man in a surf-white chiton was dancing slowly on the sand, hopping lightly from one foot to another. He was holding a flaming torch, which he waved above his head in a slow, circular motion. It wasn't a dance I had seen at any festival.

Thrax pulled me closer and I could see that the man wasn't actually dancing. He was picking his way carefully along the beach. Looking at his feet, I realised he was trying not to step on something buried in the wet sand.

He spotted us and smiled. 'Come and watch the mother goddess at her work.'

'What do you mean?' Thrax called back.

The young man lowered the torch to cast light on the wet sand. The earth around his feet was heaving like boiling water. Then something incredible happened. A small hole appeared in the sand and two little flippers reached out, followed by a head the size of a chickpea. A baby turtle was hatching, and it was not the only one. The young man swung his torch above the sand, showing us dozens of baby turtles, struggling out of a buried nest.

Above us, the harsh cry of the seagulls grew to fever pitch. Fluttering shadows swooped across the beach, getting larger by the moment.

'Help me, quickly,' cried the young man. He stuck his torch in the ground and started grabbing turtles, stuffing them down the front of his chiton.

We joined him, scooping up the wriggling creatures and placing them inside our own clothing. The noise of the seagulls became deafening as they

dived at the newborn creatures, their dreadful beaks ready for the kill.

When our chitons were bulging with squirming turtles, Thrax and I raced the young man into the waves. We waded in till the water came up to our chests, then struck out to the open sea. The hungry seagulls followed us, circling dangerously close to our heads and arms.

Once in deep water, we loosened our chitons and let the baby turtles swim free. They sank into the depths at once and the sound of the gulls faded as they rose into the air, screeching with disappointment.

'Thank you for your help,' said the young man once we had returned to the shore. In the light of his torch, his eyes were as big and dark as a wise owl's. Water streamed from his hair and wispy beard. His face was handsome but narrow, with high cheekbones and very thin eyebrows. He had a large bruise on the right side of his face and I wondered how he'd got it. Perhaps he's slipped on wet rocks and banged his face while rescuing turtles on another night. Or he might have fallen off a horse.

As he spoke, a rounded shape loomed out of the water behind us. An enormous turtle waddled up the sand. The young man stared at it with joy in his eyes. 'I believe she is the mother. Come to thank us herself.'

He cooed softly as he walked slowly towards the turtle. The ancient creature looked up at him through crinkled, wisdom-filled eyes. 'I have heard the story of Arion the poet riding a dolphin,' said the young man. 'I wonder if I might be allowed the thrill of a similar adventure too.' He clambered on to the creature's back and bent forward to whisper in her ear.

Thrax and I watched him disappear into the night, both silenced by the wonder of it all. A bright moon came out, illuminating the sea and the mountains behind us.

Sitting beside Master Ariston at festivals and symposiums, I had heard many storytellers sing the praises of Mount Parnassus. Pegasus the winged horse had once made his home on its weather-beaten rocks. The powerful nymphs were said to haunt the mountain still. The gods

Dionysus and Pan visited its caves. It was here too that the muses, the mothers of music, drama and poetry, lived, and where the god Apollo taught the poet Orpheus to play the lyre.

It looked so majestic, so awe-inspiring, with its snow-covered summit glowing in the moonlight, it was easy to believe that it was loved and protected by the gods. Nothing horrible or nasty could ever happen in its shadow. We would find no dark mystery to solve on our trip to Delphi.

As it turned out, my feeling was entirely wrong. Our next adventure had already started. Thrax and I had just failed to spot the first clue.

Or actually it was only me.

Thrax never ever misses a clue.

He is the best mystery solver in the world.

CHAPTER THREE

The Ring of the Harpies

Thrax and I resumed our hunt for charcoal. We picked up a lot of blackened wood in the forest, carrying it back to the hut in great big lumps. I woke up early the next morning and spent a pleasant hour pounding it to dust, using a flat stone. Making ink is hard work and messy but I enjoy it. It's amazing to think that something as common as burnt timber could be turned into words and sentences that carry meaning and power.

By the time I'd scooped the black powder carefully into my ink pouch, Thrax had served Master Ariston his breakfast and we were ready to go.

From Kirrha it's less than a day's journey to Delphi across the plain and up the lower slopes of Mount Parnassus. The well-used road is considered safe and is always busy. But Master Ariston has an irrational fear of wild animals and he insisted on hiring a professional guide to take us up the mountain.

The man's name was Abydos. He assured Master Ariston he would be safe in his company and we set off, Thrax and I eating our breakfast on the hoof.

Master Ariston rode sideways on Ariana, clutching his precious lyre, which Thrax had managed to repair and retune while I was making my ink. I led the donkey while Thrax brought up the rear, weighed down as always with Master Ariston's portable library.

The plain between the port of Delphi and the foot of Mount Parnassus is fertile and very well kept. There are olive groves as far as the eye can see, and their glossy leaves shone in the sunlight. The few farms we passed looked prosperous, their pens full of well fed poultry and animals. Any poet worth his salt would have been inspired by the plain's perfect beauty but Master Ariston saw danger lurking behind every bush and tree.

'Do you suppose there might be thieves in these parts?' he asked a fellow traveller when the farmland gave way to wilder countryside.

'I heard robbers are not such a threat any more,' the traveller replied. He was an extremely tall man with very dark skin and wide shoulders. His hair was cropped close to his head, as was his wiry beard. 'Athens sent hoplites to deal with them a long time ago. None have been seen since.'

'But there may be wolves,' said Master Ariston. I believe this part of the country is famous for them.'

'I don't think wolves would come out of their lairs during the day,' grinned the traveller, who was riding a chestnut horse with the glossiest coat I had ever seen. The man's name, we learned, was

Gorgias. He was a widowed merchant from a city called Sybaris on the Traeis, or New Sybaris. An old white-haired slave was travelling with him, leading a donkey weighed down with chests and rolled-up carpets.

'It's the lambing season,' grumbled Master Ariston. 'Wolves might be tempted out of their hiding places during the day by the lambs. I hope Abydos is keeping a keen eye out for them.' He looked around fearfully. 'And I hope he will use his spear the moment he sees one. I don't care if wolves are sacred to Apollo.'

Gorgias chuckled deep in his throat. 'Do not let my son Milo hear you say you want to destroy a living creature,' he said. 'He is a follower of the great Pythagoras, who insisted that all animals are sacred and have an inner spirit, just like humans. Milo insists every living creature, even something as small as a wasp or a worm, should be allowed to live as long as the gods allow it.'

'I bet he is one of those weaklings who baulks at the idea of eating meat after a sacrifice,' huffed Master Ariston, forgetting his manners.

'Milo chooses to eat only grain and vegetables,' confirmed Gorgias. 'But he is no weakling. He is a sensitive spirit who hates violence of any kind. He is also a good judge of character and does not anger easily. He and his twin brother will make fine heirs when it is my time to cross the river of the dead.'

'I will not give up meat just because a long-dead mathematician and philosopher once preferred onion to goat,' sniffed Master Ariston. 'And I certainly will not allow a rabid wolf to savage me just because it is sacred to the gods. Thrax, go and fetch our guide. I want a word with him.'

Master Ariston eyed the other pilgrims in our little caravan while Thrax went off to fetch Abydos. 'Where are your sons now?'

The merchant from Sybaris flicked the reins of his horse. 'One stayed at home to look after the business. The other, Milo, stopped at some temple or other to offer a wheat sacrifice. He will catch up with us soon. He's a very loyal son. He absolutely insisted on coming to Delphi with me.'

Abydos rode up to assure Master Ariston we were in no danger of being savaged by hungry wolves. But Master Ariston was soon complaining again, this time about the smell of dung hanging in the air.

'Thrax, my alabastron,' he wailed.

Thrax hung the small flask of perfumed oil around his master's neck. 'Ah, roses, that's better,' sniffed Master Ariston. But he was soon moaning loudly once more. He was itchy from the road dust and hungry. Besides, dark clouds were building up in the sky. It looked like it was going to rain.

The other pilgrims in the caravan, many of whom had arrived at Kirrha that very morning, suggested we should all rest for a while. Abydos took us to a wayside inn for an early meal, where Thrax set about feeding Ariana and arranging for Master Ariston to have a wash. Gorgias's slave, who was called Solon, hurried into the kitchen to see what the innkeeper and his wife could rustle up for our masters.

'May I ask why you are seeking the oracle's advice?' Master Ariston asked Gorgias once he was clean and they had settled around a rickety wooden table. The innkeeper had served them an enormous bowl of freshly cooked sprats while Thrax, Solon and I tucked into barley cakes washed down with water.

'It is a long and troubled story,' said Gorgias, 'but I am not ashamed to share it. You strike me as an honest and sensitive soul, Ariston the poet, so I will tell you.

'I am a merchant. I deal in carpets and textiles, mostly woollen cloaks made by women in my own city. My younger brother, Kosmas, was a merchant too. We learned the trade from our father. When he died, my brother and I inherited his cargo ship, a rickety but trustworthy boat that had survived many a storm at sea.

'We were young and often at loggerheads with each other. If I wanted to trade in oil, Kosmas would prefer wine. If I elected to buy grain in Egypt, he would insist on going to Samos in search of expensive pottery. I liked returning to the safety of home the moment business was concluded but Kosmas had a desire for reckless

adventure. He yearned to see more of the world, to discover new places and to experience things he could not find in our city.

'One night, after a lot of wine had been drunk, we quarrelled badly. And this time there was no going back. My brother swore never to speak to me again and we parted company. As the elder brother, I kept our father's ship and he set off to see the world, his pockets full of gold from his share of the family business.

'Freed from the distractions of my tiresome brother, I prospered as never before. In no time at all, I had a fleet of three brand-new ships. Occasionally, I got news of Kosmas from other merchants I met on my travels. Your brother is training for the games in a Spartan gym! Your brother tired of training and has opened a seafront tavern on the island of Aegina! They say he is very generous with his wine. Your brother is married and settled happily!

'Good things never lasted with Kosmas. One day, I heard that his tavern had gone bust and he had abandoned his wife. His gold had long run out and he was forced to find employment hauling cargo on a ship travelling between Egypt and Byblos.

'I often thought about trying to help him but pride and memories of our last fight always kept me from doing so. Let the gods teach him a lesson in humility, I said to myself. One day he will come crawling back and apologise for his offensive behaviour.

'Gradually, I had no more news of Kosmas. He seemed to have vanished into thin air. Then one night, I was returning to Sybaris on one of my ships. It had been a very successful voyage. The hold of my entire fleet was filled with grain and I was eager to get home to celebrate with my family.

'Passing the island of Melos, our lookout spotted a cargo ship being attacked by pirates. Its sail was on fire and it was listing badly. Usually I head for the nearest port the moment I get wind of a pirate ship but that evening something made me go to the vessel's aid. It must have been the gods whispering in my ear, for that very same night I was reunited with Kosmas.

'He lay bleeding on the deck of the cargo ship, a spear sticking out of his chest. My brother had become a pirate. His eyes grew wide when he saw me and he tried to smile.

' "Gorgias..." he began.

'A sudden burst of blood inside his mouth stopped him from saying anything more. All around us the hideous sounds of battle continued. I am a tough man who is not easily brought to tears but my heart broke as I watched him shivering uncontrollably. I knelt beside him and wiped his mouth with the hem of my chlamys.

' "Do not give up your life-spirit, Kosmas," I cried above the din of clashing spears and swords, wrapping his shoulders in my arms. "I shall take you home with me. I will make sure you get well again."

'My brother coughed and more blood and foam spluttered out of his mouth. "It is too late, Gorgias. I have been speared like a fish." He held up a trembling hand to show me a ring on his middle finger. It was dripping with my own brother's blood.

'"I have a daughter, Gorgias," he said. "She lives with her mother, a priestess of Hera on the island of Aegina. Find her and give her this. It is the only thing I have in the world."

'I cradled his head on my lap. "You will give it to her yourself, Kosmas," I cried. "You will survive and see your daughter again."

'He gripped the hem of my himation with the last bit of strength left in him. "I die, brother. I die! But keep your word. Give this ring to my daughter or the gods will call the curse of the harpies upon you as Zeus did with King Phineus."

'That was the last thing my brother ever said to me. A moment later his grip on my himation loosened and he fell back dead. By then my men and the sailors on the cargo ship had driven the pirates back on to their own vessel. I wanted to take Kosmas home for a proper burial but pirates are always buried at sea, for they believe that Dionysus turns their shades into dolphins.

'I only had a moment to tug the ring off Kosmas's finger before they took the body away. As I wiped off the blood, I realised it was a piece of jewellery fit for a king. A wide band of gold topped with two angry harpies glaring at each other. Their eyes were little beads of precious carnelian, as red as the blood I had just wiped off them. Who knows where Kosmas had come across it or who he had stolen it from?'

'And did you return it to your brother's daughter as promised?' asked Master Ariston breathlessly, dying to know how the incredible story ended.

'My brother's mind must have been wandering when I spoke to him on the deck of that ship,' said Gorgias. 'He must have given me the name of the wrong island. When I went to Aegina, I found no priestess with a child from an unknown father. The search for my niece continues.'

Master Ariston thumped the table with his fist, wincing at the pain. 'And now you intend to ask the oracle where the child might be.'

Gorgias nodded at Solon, who refilled his wine cup. 'Sadly, I have a more pressing question. You see, I am afraid that despite my best intentions to fulfill my promise to Kosmas, I shall soon be cursed by the harpies. I shall be like King Phineus all those years ago.'

'But why?' asked Master Ariston.

The merchant looked around his little group of listeners. 'Even if I did find my niece, I cannot give her the ring. It has been stolen from my purse. That is the question I intend to ask the oracle: Where can I find the ring of the harpies?'

CHAPTER FOUR

Trouble at the Cheesemaker's

A shadow fell across the table and we all looked up to see a thin figure silhouetted in the doorway.

'Ah,' said Gorgias, a fatherly smile spreading across his face. 'Here is my son Milo at last.'

The figure parted the flimsy curtain and stepped into the room. It was the young man Thrax and I had met on the beach.

'A pleasant morning,' he mumbled, nodding to each of us in turn before taking his place at the table. He smiled at Thrax and myself but made no mention of our adventure with the turtles the night before. Perhaps he was trying to be discreet in case we hadn't asked for permission to wander so far out of town.

Milo poured himself a glass of wine before Solon could do it for him and added water from a pitcher. I warmed to him at once. Here was a wealthy man who didn't expect to be waited on hand and foot.

'Do you want something to eat, son?' said Gorgias.

'Just bread, and perhaps a bit of cheese if they have it,' replied Milo, rubbing the bruise on the side of his face. 'Olives will do if they haven't.'

Solon hurried away to fetch the food, taking the remains of the sprats with him in case their smell offended Milo.

Abydos wanted Master Ariston to get his first glimpse of Delphi at sunset, so we stayed on at the inn for a while before continuing our journey.

As we travelled up the mountain, the plain fell away behind us. The sky cleared without releasing a downpour and started to turn red from the setting sun. It became eerily silent save for the call of wild birds and the rushing of water in the springs.

Delphi remained hidden from view till we came round an enormous stony crag. And then, as if by godly magic, it was suddenly revealed in all its glory. The marble of the famous temple glowed in the sunset as if on fire. A giant statue of Apollo stared back at us with glowing polished-marble eyes.

Towering behind the city but dwarfed by the might of Mount Parnassus stood two enormous cliff-like rocks with a ravine between them.

'They are called the Phaedriades,' explained Abydos. 'A river flows down the mountain to form a spring between them. They call it the Castalian spring, and athletes at the Pythian Games wash themselves in it before they compete.'

'I'd love to watch the Pythian Games,' said Thrax. 'They say the athletes who do well here go on to win crowns at Olympia.'

'They took place last year.' Abydos led us through the crowds. 'But if you want to visit the oracle you still have to purify yourself at the Castalian spring before you see the Pythia.'

'Ah, Delphi! Delphi!' sighed Master Ariston as we entered the city. 'A place special to Apollo and the muses. So inspiring for a writer like me...'

The god speaks through the oracle on the seventh day of each month. We had arrived in Delphi two days early but the city was already packed with pilgrims. Abydos led us to a roomy and well-appointed inn on the main street. Master Ariston's Athenian accent bagged him a room with views of the Phaedriades. As Master Aristion explained later, Athenian pilgrims bring a lot of money to Delphi and are always given preferential treatment. Gorgias's gold got him and Milo a smaller room looking out on to the courtyard.

Solon, Thrax and I were given sleeping space in a backyard. I swear it was no bigger than my wax tablet. Judging by the piles of rotting vegetables, it was the spot where the cook threw out his scraps. Even as we looked, the mound of rubbish quivered and a small furry face appeared.

'This place is overrun with vermin,' said Thrax. 'There may be snakes as well as mice. And it might rain during the night. I'm not sleeping here. Come on, Nico, let's find some kind spirit who'll let us sleep in a clean barn or a shed. We could offer to do odd jobs in return.'

'Won't Master Ariston mind if we sleep away from the inn?'

Thrax nodded up at a window where Master Ariston's snoring had started to shake the walls. 'Listen to that. He won't notice even if the inn falls down around his ears. Let's go.'

We ventured out into Delphi, wearing our himations against the cold mountain air. Even though we urgently needed to find somewhere to sleep, we couldn't help but be distracted by the sight of the famous sanctuary of Apollo.

I am not yet skilled enough as a writer to describe the magnificence of it. The huge temple sits on a specially built platform, surrounded by columns. All around it stand priceless statues on pedestals. They are gifts to the sanctuary from grateful cities and important people. There is one

of a young man driving a horse-drawn chariot. Another shows a sphinx with pointed wings. Some of the monuments are enormous bronze tripods, the symbols of Delphi itself. Towering above them all is the giant statue of Apollo we saw as we approached the city.

The Sacred Way, the path taken by the pilgrims, snakes its way through the sanctuary towards the temple. It is flanked by treasure houses filled with gold and precious objects.

'We don't have time to look at them tonight,' said Thrax. 'Unless you want to sleep on a mouse-infested rubbish heap.'

Reluctantly, I followed him away from the sanctuary. Compared to Corinth, or even Athens, Delphi seemed to be a very tidy city. A place truly worthy of the gods. The streets were clean, the roadside shrines and houses well looked after.

'The great Apollo does indeed bless this place,' I said.

'You mean running a famous oracle makes a lot of money,' chuckled Thrax.

We came to a crowded agora with colonnades around the perimeter. Thrax spied a street vendor and we bought a hot sausage each, wolfing it down as we explored the market. I spotted Milo in the crowd. He was hurrying along with another man in a hood. I raised my hand in greeting but Milo did not see us and walked on. He and his friend seemed eager to escape the crowd.

After our delicious supper, we left the market and came to a poorer part of town, with smaller houses and narrower, dirtier streets. A milky smell hung in the air, making me wrinkle my nose.

'I recognise this smell from the farm I worked on,' said Thrax. 'There must be a cheesemaker nearby.'

We turned a corner and spotted a small establishment at the far end of a yard. It was still open. An old man with a scuffed leather apron was scrubbing the threshold with a stiff brush.

'Good evening,' said Thrax as we approached.

The cheesemaker, who had a kind face as leathery as his apron, struggled to his feet.

'Looking for some cheese for your master, lads?'

'We're looking for somewhere dry and warm to sleep,' said Thrax. 'We can't pay in cash but we'll do odd jobs instead.'

The cheesemaker looked us up and down with watery eyes. 'Where are you from?'

'Athens,' I replied.

'Are you pilgrims?'

'Our master is,' answered Thrax. 'But there's no room for us at the inn.'

'There's never room for the slaves and servants,' sighed the cheesemaker. 'Well, you can sleep in my cheese shop if you want. You look like honest lads to me. There've been kids fighting on the streets around here at night and I'm worried they might break into my shop. I could do with someone keeping an eye on the place. You'll save me the fee for a city guard. People tell me it's a bit smelly in here, but I've been around it so long I never notice the stink. I dare say you boys will soon get used to it. The embers are still warm in the hearth. Better than catching your death sleeping outdoors.'

'It's a deal,' said Thrax. He stuck out his right hand, which the cheesemaker shook limply.

He nodded at a crumbling house outside the yard. 'I live across the street. If you hear anyone coming in the night, just shout. The wife will hear you and wake me up. Good night.' He patted a statue of Aristaios, the god of cheesemaking, before shutting the gate to the yard behind him.

When he was gone, Thrax and I stepped into the shop, which seemed much bigger inside than it looked from the outside. There were shelves all around the walls, piled high with little round cheeses.

The place wasn't 'a bit smelly,' as the cheesemaker had claimed. It stank to the heavens. Still, the sight of all that delicious cheese made my stomach rumble with hunger, despite the sausage I had just eaten.

'Don't you dare even THINK about it,' warned Thrax, spreading his himation close to the smouldering fire. 'The man trusted us. We can't steal from an honest worker.'

Reluctantly, I turned my gaze away from all the goods on display and put down my himation near Thrax's. The journey to Delphi had taken its toll and soon I was fast asleep with my toes close to the glowing embers. I was in the middle of a luscious dream where I was sharing cheese and nectar with the gods, when Thrax shook me awake.

'Nico! Get up. I heard the gate creak open. There's someone in the yard.'

Shaking the muzziness out of my head, I got up and tiptoed after him to the doorway. We crouched there out of sight as a dark figure closed the gate behind it and stepped into the middle of the yard. It looked around for a moment, the shawl covering its head swinging from side to side. Then it darted to the altar of Aristaios and crouched out of sight behind it.

A few moments later we heard loud, rough voices and the gate was kicked open with so much force it crashed against the wall.

'Khaire,' yelled a boisterous voice. 'We know you're in here, fire-hair.'

A boy around my age, but much brawnier, stepped into the yard. He had a very sweaty face with puffy cheeks and almost no eyebrows. His hair stood up in big oily tufts on his head. A short himation swirled round his chubby ankles and he was wielding a wooden club.

Behind him stood perhaps six or seven children, all peering around them with a hard look in their eyes and a sneer on their mouths. None of them carried clubs like their leader but a few had their fists balled ready for a fight, or a beating.

'Is she in here, Belos?'

'Come out and face us, harpy,' called one of them.

'Yeah,' added another. 'How come your face never burns when your hair is always on fire? Ha, ha, ha.'

A wave of cruel laughter rippled through the gang. 'Come out and get your *punishment*. You know you shouldn't trespass into the agora, gorgon. That's *our* territory. Boy's territory. Girls are only allowed in the bit that sells cooking pots.'

One of the boys spotted the figure behind the altar. 'There she is, Belos. Hiding like a true gorgon, waiting to pounce.'

'Ha, ha, she is even scarier than a gorgon.'

The boys moved towards the altar as one, like a pack of vicious wolves closing in on a helpless fawn. I heard the sound of ripping as they tore the epiblema from her shoulder and her face was revealed. For a moment I thought I was looking at a goddess. The girl's skin was almost white, like a marble statue before it's painted. Her hair was, as the boys had said, a fiery red. She glared back at Belos with the fiercest green eyes I had ever seen. And then spat straight in his face.

Belos was so shocked, he froze. A gasp rippled through the rest of the gang.

'Hey,' said Thrax, stepping out of the doorway before Belos could react. 'Leave that girl alone. Find someone your own size to pick on.'

Belos turned round to face us, the girl's spittle dribbling down his face. 'Who dares stick up for the gorgon?'

'No one we know, Belos,' said a boy who had pimples all over his face. 'Just some stranger.'

'Strangers don't come to Delphi and tell us what to do,' sneered Belos. He wiped away the spittle and chewed his fat lower lip. 'Come on. Let's teach the gorgon a lesson. And then we'll see about the... pilgrims.' He spat out this last word to make it sound like an insult.

The next thing I knew, Thrax had leapt forward, his muscles taut and veiny. His shaved head met Belos's stomach full on and they both rolled over in the dust. A money bag under the boy's himation split under the impact and shiny coins scattered in the dust. There was a cheer as some of the younger boys forgot about the fight and made a dive for them.

The rest turned away from the girl and surrounded Thrax. I have to confess that fighting scares me. I am no good with fists and kicking feet. But there was no way I was going to let

Thrax take a beating on his own. So I let out a loud yell (or at least I tried yelling; the sound that came out of my mouth was more like a mousy squeak) and hurled myself straight into the fray.

Before my feet had even touched the ground, I got two dizzying knocks on the head and a wallop full in the face. It sent me reeling out on to the street.

'Boys, are you all right?' boomed a voice above me.

A light appeared in the window of the cheesemaker's house and a dog started barking madly.

None of the others even heard the roar. The fighting followed me out on to the street, with Thrax in the middle of it. I could see him lashing out with the fierceness of Hercules attacking the Nemean lion. He had that glazed, angry look in his eyes that I had seen the first night I met him, when he'd had a nightmare about his long-lost mother.

More lights appeared in windows across the street.

'Knock it off, you hoodlums,' someone roared angrily. 'I have to get up for work soon.'

'Why don't you go and fight in your own street? Bother your own parents, if you have any. Mutts!'

The gang dragged Thrax towards a fountain and Belos forced his head under the water.

'Help,' I yelled at the open windows. 'They're going to drown my friend.'

I had no more opportunity to shout because a moment later, something thick and slimy splattered all over me, drenching me from head to toe. It stank and I realised with horror that people in the nearby houses were emptying their chamber pots on us.

I was not the only victim. Many in the gang were dripping wet too, Belos's tufty hair was plastered to his head with pee. Howling in outrage, he let go of Thrax and hurled his club at a window. It fell short, making the people in the houses on either side of the street jeer and laugh.

'If I still had my health, I'd come down and sort you out,' growled the cheesemaker. 'I know

61

who you are. If I ever see you round this part of town again, I'll have a word with your master. You'll be out of a job.'

Belos kicked the cheesermaker's door to show he wasn't scared by threats. 'Come on, gang,' he hissed, his eyes red with rage and shame. 'Let's go. We'll deal with the girl and these pilgrims some other time.'

A boy handed him his club and the gang ran off into the night.

Thrax turned to me. 'Are you all right, Nico?' The mad look had disappeared from his eyes but a vein on his forehead was still throbbing.

'I'll be all right once I've cleaned myself up,' I said, trying not to vomit at the sight of a big fat turd plastered to the front of my chiton. 'I smell like a cesspit.'

'You look like a cesspit too,' Thrax laughed. Somehow he'd evaded being hit by the contents of the chamber pots and his chiton was still spotless. But his left eye was beginning to swell. He was going to have a glorious shiner by morning.

'What about the girl?' I said.

Thrax dashed back into the cheesemaker's yard while I took off my chiton and shook away the turd. But the mysterious girl with red hair had vanished.

CHAPTER FIVE

A Puzzling Symposium

Master Ariston's jaw dropped when he saw us early the next morning. Thrax's left eye had swollen like a loaf of bread before it goes in the oven. My bashed lips were almost as bad and my chin was redder than an onion in a stew.

'What in the name of Zeus happened to you two?' he gasped, sitting up in bed. 'Are there wild boars in the backyard?'

'No, but there are mice,' said Thrax. 'And possibly snakes and scorpions. It's not safe to sleep there. We found a cheesemaker who let us spend the night in his shop.'

'Only, we were attacked by a gang of local boys,' I added.

'Serves you right for creeping out of the inn without my permission,' sniffed Master Ariston. 'Help me get dressed, Thrax. I shall have breakfast with the other pilgrims downstairs.'

The innkeeper greeted Master Ariston with a grovelling nod and tiganites – wheat pancakes topped with honey.

'A message for you has come from one of the great archons of Delphi, an official in the sanctuary,' he said. 'It was delivered by one of his slaves this morning.'

Master Ariston's face lit up at the news. 'A message from a magistrate? How wonderful. What did it say?'

The innkeeper cleared his throat. 'Glykon has heard that Ariston, the son of Lykos the retired sea captain, is in Delphi and invites him to dinner this evening. He will send a slave to escort Ariston and his retinue to his house just after sunset.'

'My fame precedes me,' beamed Master Ariston through a mouth full of figs and pancake. 'Glykon might help me get in to see the Pythia. Go and brush down my clothes, Thrax, and do something about your faces, both of you. I can't have my retinue looking like a gang of common criminals.'

'I'll bring my writing tools in case you are inspired, sir,' I said.

'I am going as a guest not a performer,' sniffed Master Ariston. 'But I suppose you should bring parchment and papyrus. It will make me look rich.'

The sun had barely set when the archon's slave arrived and led us across town. Glykon's house was modest from the outside, with a small altar of Hermes by the front door such as you would find in Athens. But inside, the andron was lavishly decorated with a mosaic floor and statues of athletes. The archon welcomed us as we removed our sandals and a slave bathed Master Ariston's feet.

'Khaire! Greetings to our visitor from Athens. We are quite a far-flung gathering tonight. We have a merchant and his son from New Sybaris coming too. I believe you know them already.'

Glykon invited Master Ariston to recline on a couch piled high with cushions while Thrax and I took our positions behind it, hoping our facial injuries would not be noticed. If they were, no one was rude enough to mention them. Gorgias and Milo came in, and then more guests, till nearly all the couches in the andron were full. They washed their hands as slaves poured water on them. Then Glykon clapped twice and other slaves ran in to fill the place with small tables.

'I say, this food looks delicious,' said Master Ariston, watching the slaves cover the tables with piping-hot dishes. He raised his cup at Gorgias who was sharing a couch with Milo. 'Although you might not be impressed, sir. I hear the people of New Sybaris are famous for their extravagant dining.'

'They might be,' chuckled Gorgias, holding up his own cup in greeting, 'but as a seaman myself, I prefer simpler food like this.'

Milo sipped from his wine cup thoughtfully and did not join in the conversation. He had the same distant look in his eye that Thrax gets when he's thinking hard and I wondered what was on his mind.

There was a commotion outside the andron and a late guest was shown in. He was a tall man, with broad shoulders and a long beard flecked with grey.

'I do apologise for my late arrival,' the guest said to Glykon as slaves rushed to remove his sandals and chlamys. 'I was held up over an important matter at the temple.'

'There is no need to apologise,' Glykon assured him. 'Let me introduce you to some of my guests. This is Ariston, a famous poet from Athens. This is Gorgias from New Sybaris who has come to petition the oracle with his son Milo. Gentlemen, this is my friend Abantes, who became one of the priests at the sanctuary a few months ago.'

'Greetings,' said Master Ariston while the slaves piled cushions on an empty couch for

Abantes to sit on. 'You have come just in time to share some delicious food.'

Abantes waited for a slave to put a small table in front of his couch and plump up the cushions before sitting down. 'So you are a poet,' he said.

'And a performer too,' answered Master Ariston. 'Although I am not entertaining tonight.'

Abantes watched a slave pour wine into his kylix. 'And what trade are you in?' he asked Gorgias.

'I am a merchant,' said Gorgias. 'As are my twin sons. We deal in carpets and textiles.'

Abantes held out a small dish of anchovies that a slave had placed before him. Gorgias scooped up some of the food with a piece of bread. 'You'll have to excuse my son,' he said. 'He is not being rude. He does not eat fish or meat. He is an admirer of Pythagoras.'

Abantes passed the dish to Master Ariston. 'I have never met a man who refuses to eat flesh before, although I hear there is a growing number of them. Most of the people in the world can't afford to eat meat. It's a shame we turn it down when the gods themselves provide it for us. Still, I am pleased to meet you, young man.'

'And what do you do for a living when you are not officiating at the sanctuary, sir?' asked Master Ariston.

'I used to be a soldier,' said Abantes. 'But I retired when I was wounded in the leg. My family come from Aegina. My father was a goldsmith there before he passed away.'

'You must like Delphi very much to make it your home,' said Master Ariston, reaching for some food.

'I think it is the best place in the world,' replied Abantes. 'I visited here with a general who consulted the oracle fourteen years ago. I fell in love with it then, and have always wanted to come back for good.'

Master Ariston gulped down his food. 'Did you bring your family with you?'

'Sadly, I'm a widower,' said Abantes, chewing on his lower lip. 'I am all alone in the world.'

'But Aegina too is a special place,' cried Gorgias. 'The island of turtles. I have been there before on personal business. I take it you have worshipped at the famous temple of Aphaia there, sir?'

Master Ariston, who was already on his third cup of wine, interrupted the conversation again. 'As a lover of golden jewellery, sir, I could not help but notice the fibula on your chlamys, shaped like Artemis's bow. Is it your father's work?'

'No,' replied Abantes, scowling. 'I bought this in Delphi a few days ago. I did have a beautiful one my father made me when I joined the navy, a memento of him and Aegina, but sadly I lost it.'

He changed the subject of the conversation and the men's talk turned to sport and war. More food was brought in till no one could eat another mouthful. The second part of the symposium was announced. Perhaps because he'd been so quiet all evening, Milo was chosen to be 'king of the festivities' and to decide how much water should go in the wine.

Gorgias beamed with pride as Milo kicked off the proceedings by proposing a toast to Zeus. 'Isn't he a good public speaker?' he said to Abantes.

'Yes, he is,' the priest replied. 'You must introduce me to your son properly.'

The guests put on garlands and settled down to an evening of music, storytelling and games. Thrax and I had watched these so many times we had stopped finding them exciting a long time ago.

'Let's sneak into the kitchen and see if we can get some food,' I whispered as Gorgias started telling a rude story from Sybaris. 'Looking at people eating always makes me hungry. There may be some sardines or anchovies left.'

The two of us slipped unnoticed out of the andron. There was no fish left in the kitchen but the cook gave us cake and fruit. Thrax was very quiet while we ate and I knew he was thinking very hard.

He'd found something at the symposium very puzzling.

CHAPTER SIX

The Oracle's Advice

'Help me get dressed, Thrax,' barked Master Ariston. 'My best chiton and boots, please. I can't show up at the most famous oracle in the world wearing rags.'

'There must be hundreds of people trying to see the Pythia today,' I said. 'Do you think Glykon will manage to get you in?'

Master Ariston grinned slyly. 'I promised him that my father would send a generous gift from Athens. Besides, Athens and Delphi have a special agreement. Important Athenians can jump to the front of the queue, for a price. That's why the Athenian treasure house in the sanctuary is bursting with gold. I hope my new friend Gorgias will get in too. That poor man is going mad with worry about his lost ring.'

Consulting the oracle is a tiring process that can take all day. There's a lot of waiting about, consulting with priests and temple officials, praying and offering sacrifice. Thrax and I were told to wait outside the sanctuary and the sun was setting by the time Master Ariston came out. He was beaming from ear to ear.

'What did the oracle foretell?' I asked as we hurried back to the inn through the streets of Delphi.

'The priestess does not speak in a tongue you and I would understand,' said Master Ariston. 'She speaks the language of the gods, which is a horrible sound like nothing I have ever heard in my life. She sits on a tripod in the dark, surrounded by thick smoke made by burning branches of laurel and oleander. Very soon you can hardly see anything for that choking smoke.

It gets in your eyes and makes your throat as dry as desert sand.

'When you call out your question, though how anyone can be expected to speak in that choking smoke I don't know, the Pythia listens. Then she closes her eyes and starts rocking to and fro on her seat as the god whispers in her ear. I must admit the whole process made my skin crawl. I don't frighten easily as you know, boys, but this was quite scary.

'The Pythia's rocking gets more frantic. She flails wildly with her hands. She moans and raves until she is foaming at the mouth like a poisoned horse. I suppose having direct contact with the power of the gods does that to you. Then she leaps to her feet and I swear by the mighty Apollo, when she opens her eyes again, the pupils have turned purple.'

'You must have imagined that last bit, master,' said Thrax. 'No one's pupils can change colour.'

'I tell you I saw it myself,' insisted Master Ariston. 'Her eyes were as purple as Phoenician cloth. All at once her raving stopped and she slumped forward so that temple assistants had to rush to stop her from crashing to the floor. It was very intense and dramatic.'

'But did she answer your question?' I asked. We had by now reached the inn and Master Ariston slumped into a moth-eaten couch. Thrax poured him some water and wine.

'Oh yes! Abantes the priest had been standing close to the Pythia's stool while she raved. He has the gift of understanding what the priestess's ranting means and he wrote the god's message down for me.'

'And what advice did the oracle give you?' I asked.

Master Ariston held out a tablet and I read the message written neatly in the wax:

Turning a corner in life, the poet shall come across a sea of merriment.

'Isn't it wonderful?' he cried. 'It's just what I wanted to hear.' He traced his fingers along the writing. 'Turning a corner in life is a poetic way of saying changing direction. And that's what I am doing, isn't it? Switching from the calling of a travelling poet to the higher one of playwright. And the sea of merriment must mean an audience cheering for my writing. The oracle foresees a glorious future in comedy for me.'

He held up the tablet and kissed it with pure joy in his eyes.

'Boys, I've decided we're staying on in Delphi for a while. I am going to write my first proper play here. Oh, I know I dabbled with writing a few dramatic scenes in Corinth but this is going to be a major work. A side-splitting comedy as the oracle instructed. And first thing tomorrow morning, I am going to a barber's to have my hair and beard styled to make me look like a proper playwright.'

CHAPTER SEVEN

A Tree House

The day after the oracle had spoken, most of the pilgrims left the city. A river of people flowed down the mountain towards the port at Kirrha and the main road to Athens. The only strangers left in Delphi were rich men who had not managed to get an audience with the oracle and had decided to stay on till the next big day.

Gorgias was one of these. We found him sitting morosely in the dining room. Milo was seated beside him, sipping thoughtfully from a cup.

'Were you not chosen to consult the Pythia?' asked Master Ariston kindly.

Gorgias glowered at the food in front of him. 'I can't understand what happened. We threw dice to see who would get in and my number came up. I had even paid for my honey cake, the tribute you must leave on the altar. But right at the last moment the priests hustled someone else into the presence of the Pythia instead of me. A very important general from Sparta.'

'How humiliating for you,' said Master Ariston. 'Being told to give up your place in the queue, and in front of so many important people. I take it you are going to stay on till the seventh of next month?'

'I suggested to Father that he consult one of the priests at the temple,' said Milo. 'They are also seers.'

Gorgias spat out his bread. 'I didn't come all the way from Sybaris to watch some local priest fiddle with dice or knucklebones,' he spluttered. 'I must have the advice of the great Pythia herself.

I want a message straight from the mouth of the god.'

Milo placed a hand on his father's arm to calm him down. 'We'll wait if that's what you want, Father.' He turned to Master Ariston. 'I hear you are staying on in Delphi too, to write a play.'

Master Ariston grinned. 'News travels fast in this town. Yes, I am staying on till I finish my first masterpiece. I'm writing a hilarious comedy based on the famous legend of how Apollo brought the first priests to Delphi disguised as a dolphin. You two must be my guests on opening night.'

Speaking as a writer myself, I couldn't see how Master Ariston could turn such a holy legend into a comedy. But it wasn't my place to criticize. Merely to write down what my employer dictated.

'Are you staying on with us at the inn?' asked Gorgias. 'We could play board games by the fire in the evening. I enjoy a game of tavli.'

'Oh no,' replied Master Ariston. 'It's far too noisy here to write, even when the town is half empty. I can't have any distractions. The boys and I are going to be staying in a country house just outside Delphi. The owners are friends of my father, from Athens. I spoke to the man who looks after it. He agreed on their behalf to let me rent it.'

'I should imagine they'll be charging you a fortune for a house in such an idyllic spot,' said Gorgias, pushing away his half-eaten food.

'Ha! I'm not parting with an obol,' laughed Master Ariston, whose great love for money was dwarfed only by his reluctance to spend it. 'They have an orchard with fruit trees and beehives. They also keep rabbits and hens. Thrax is going to look after everything for them instead of payment.'

I saw Thrax go red in the face at the news. Master Ariston had not even discussed the matter with him.

'Oh?' exclaimed Gorgias, noticing Thrax's red face and winking slyly.

'Thrax used to live on a farm before he came to me,' explained Master Ariston, completely oblivious to his slave's feelings. 'He loves getting his hands dirty. We're going to have a lovely time.'

* * *

We moved into the country house that very same day. It looked very much like an Athenian dwelling except it had no neighbours. In Athens, even rich men's houses are squashed together on smelly, narrow streets. The noise is constant. Here the only sound was the wind in the trees, and the buzzing of bees in the orchard behind the house. There were three enormous hives, placed under the olive trees so that the bees could feast on the spring blossom.

Thrax soon got the hang of looking after them and collecting the honey, which a farmer called Heliodorus came to pick up. I was kept busy writing down Master Ariston's play for several days, with breaks only for meals and short walks in the countryside.

The man in charge of the house had arranged for Heliodorus and his family to cook and deliver our meals as well as pick up the honey. For a fee so pitiful even Master Ariston could not refuse, they would keep us supplied with sausages, bean stews, lentil dishes, vegetables, fruit, nuts and wine.

These were delivered by the farmer's elder daughter, Zoe. She was a beautiful, plump girl, with fists bigger than Thrax's, and she walked with her back held straight, like all mountain people. She seemed to take a shine to Thrax and her eyes sparkled every time he talked to her. I tried not to feel jealous every time she ignored me.

'Master Ariston said you have a younger sister,' I said one morning to get her attention. She had come to deliver fresh bread and a huge goatskin of wine, which she carried slung over her back. 'How come we never see her?'

'Selene is always busy in spring and summer,' replied Zoe, smiling at Thrax as if he'd asked the question. 'She makes honey cakes for pilgrims to sacrifice at the sanctuary, and when the oracle is not open she takes the goats up the mountain. The grass is lusher up there in the dry seasons. It helps the goats make thicker milk. She's rarely at home.'

Our quiet life outside Delphi rolled on. Master Ariston's play progressed from scene to scene and my fingers grew blisters from holding the reed pen so long. I hardly saw Thrax, who was busy looking after the orchard and the bees. The spring flowers were now open, and the countryside was heady with their scent.

One evening, I came back from a walk with Master Ariston to find Thrax covered from head to toe in wood chippings. His eyes were bright with excitement. 'I have a surprise for you.'

I put my pens in a pot of water to clean. 'A surprise?'

'Come out to the orchard, but I have to cover your eyes.'

Laughing, we stumbled out of the back gate. I could hear the bees in the hives and the hens clucking in the coop. We stopped and Thrax removed his hands from my face.

'Do you like it?'

'Oh,' I gasped, lost for words.

Thrax had built a tree house in the branches of an ancient olive tree. There were two platforms to serve as cots, with old himations spread over them for mattresses. A full goatskin and a small lamp hung above each bed, and there was a shelf next to my cot for my tablet and pens. A piece of old sailcloth was stretched among the higher branches to keep off the rain.

'Thanks, Thrax,' I said, moved by his generosity. 'This is wonderful.'

'Now we can sleep outdoors without the fear of vermin or snakes. Just like I did on the farm outside Thebes,' he said, adding wood to a smouldering fire in a cracked hydria on the ground. 'And this will keep the wolves away.'

I went to bed very happy and content that night. The tree house was magical, like something out of an old legend. The spring nights were still cold but wrapped up in my himation, watching the fire, I felt a warm glow spread inside me. The wood Thrax had put in the cracked hydria was olive and its luxurious scent filled the air. Ariana snored softly the pen nearby. Master Ariston snored loudly indoors and the doves cooed on the roof.

I looked up at the multitude of stars in the sky and sighed blissfully. 'Now if only we had a little mystery to solve, a small burglary perhaps or someone wanting us to find a lost pet. Life would be perfect.'

CHAPTER EIGHT

Missing

When I stumbled bleary-eyed into the house the next morning, I found Master Ariston glowering at the table.

'There's only a crust of bread left for breakfast,' he grumbled. 'And it's hard as rock.'

'Hasn't Zoe been with fresh supplies?' I asked.

'Not yet,' said Thrax, who was combing Master Ariston's hair.

'She's never late,' I said. 'Perhaps she's been held up with some urgent matter.'

'You mean's she's forgotten,' fumed Master Ariston. 'The silly girl! She's more interested in making eyes at Thrax than serving me, who's paying her.'

Thrax ignored this last remark.

'You two had better go and fetch the food yourselves,' said Master Ariston. 'I can't run the risk of having no lunch. It's impossible to write funny scenes on an empty stomach. We're out of water too.'

I get annoyed when Master Ariston treats me like a slave. He always seems to forget I'm freeborn. My job is to write, not to fetch and carry. But I like being out with Thrax, so I put on my himation and slung an empty goatskin over my shoulder.

In Athens, your neighbours live so close to you, you can hear them talking through the walls. But here on Mount Parnassus, visiting your neighbour meant a pleasant walk in the fresh mountain air with the sound of birdsong in your ears.

'Hey,' said Thrax as we reached Heliodorus's farm. 'Whatever is going on?'

The front door to the house was wide open and a long, high-pitched wailing came from inside. There was the sound of pottery being smashed on the floor, followed by the roar of an angry man.

Zoe had seen us through the open door and came rushing out. 'I'm sorry for not bringing food this morning, Thrax. We are frantic with worry. My sister Selene has run away.'

Heliodorus, a thickset man with a very brown wrinkled face, strode out of the house and pushed his daughter aside to get past. His eyes were red with anger and his hands were balled up in fists as if he wanted a fight.

He whistled and a Spartan hound padded out from behind a tree, its tongue hanging out of its mouth. Heliodorus mumbled something as he stopped to rub its ears, then master and dog marched on without looking back. Together they disappeared down the path.

'I apologise for his rude behaviour,' said Zoe. 'He hides his fear with rage. He is very worried about Selene.'

'Where do you think she has run off to?' asked Thrax.

'My mother thinks she has gone to the mountains,' said Zoe. 'There are caves up there where she can hide.'

A thin, reedy voice called from inside the house. 'Thugater!'

'Please, come in,' said Zoe. 'My mother wishes to speak to you.'

Thrax and I followed her. The farmhouse seemed to have only one room, with extremely tiny windows that let in the light but kept out thieves and vandals. It was spotless, with a fire burning in one corner and cooking utensils arranged neatly on a wooden shelf. Beneath it were two beds with clean mattresses. The farmer's wife was rocking backwards and forwards on a stool in front of a small household altar showing Hera, the goddess of the family. Her fingers clutched a woollen epiblema on her lap.

She smiled through her tears when she saw us. The rocking stopped. 'Please, get our visitors some milk,' she said to Zoe, who had started clearing away the broken pottery.

I flinched at the thought of drinking raw milk, for in Athens only barbarians are believed to do so. Cultured people only have it in cheese. Thrax, on the other hand, drained his cup in one gulp.

The farmer's wife managed a weak grin. 'I can tell you were brought up in the country. Farm people understand how good fresh milk is. My Selene likes her milk too.'

Thrax put down his cup and wiped his mouth with the back of his hand. 'When did she run away?'

'Yesterday.' The farmer's wife clutched the epiblema to her chest. 'She had an argument with her father about going out on her own again. We don't mind her taking the goats to pasture in spring and summer. Many girls around here do that. But she keeps going into town too, without her sister Zoe as a chaperone. It's not proper for girls to do that, even farmers' daughters. The boys jeer at her. She is becoming the laughing stock of Delphi. We are a good family and our children must behave accordingly. Selene has a fine chance of being chosen to be a Pythia when she's older. She must show she is a respectable girl or she'll have no future.'

These last words made the farmer's wife dissolve into a fresh bout of sobbing. An enormous tear rolled down her weather-beaten cheek.

'Please,' she begged, holding trembling hands out to Thrax. 'I was about to send Zoe to fetch you. We've heard you are a kind and resourceful boy. Find my daughter. Tell her to come back to her family. Her father might be very strict but that's because he loves her very much.'

'Your master told my parents all about your adventure in Corinth when he came to hire us,' explained Zoe. 'She's hoping you can come to Selene's rescue too.'

The farmer's wife fumbled inside her dress and pulled out a small purse. 'We make a little from selling goats to the temple. We can pay.'

Thrax pushed the bag away gently. 'I couldn't take money from you poor, working folk. But I'll help find your daughter. She will come back home.'

The farmer's wife wiped away the tear and reached out to ruffle Thrax's hair. 'Thank you. May the gods bless you and your friend.'

Thrax pulled a stool close to the farmer's wife and sat down. 'I need to ask you some questions,' he said. 'You must answer as accurately as you can. What time did the argument happen?'

'The sun had not yet set. I was laying out our evening meal.'

'And did Selene run away straight after the argument?'

The farmer's wife shook her head. 'We don't know. We just found her bed empty this morning. It hadn't been slept in.'

'The weather's been nice these last few days. How can you be sure that she's not just out on the mountain pastures?' I asked.

'She left the goats behind,' explained Zoe. 'Selene would never go up the mountain without them, not unless she knew she wasn't coming back. My father knows this mountain like the back of his hand and he's not found her. That's why he looked so angry and upset just now.'

'So where do you think she went?' asked Thrax. 'Could she have gone down the mountain to Kirrha?'

Zoe frowned. 'No one in our family has ever been there except my father, and he only went once, a long time ago, to buy goats.'

'Could Selene be staying with friends in the city?' said Thrax.

'Selene has no friends. She's a loner.'

Thrax indicated the beds. 'Does your sister sleep in here?'

'No,' replied Zoe. 'These beds are mine and my mother's. My father sleeps on a cot in the big barn in case someone tries to steal the animals. We have a smaller barn, a shed really. Selene sleeps in there.'

'May we have a look?' said Thrax.

Zoe led us out of a back door across an orchard. I was expecting a dirty hovel but the shed was surprisingly clean. The walls were painted a fresh white and there was a wooden door with a carved handle. Zoe pulled it open. 'Has anyone been in here since Selene ran away?' asked Thrax.

'Father sent me to look but I didn't need to go past the doorway to know that Selene wasn't in here. There's nowhere for her to hide.'

Thrax peered inside the shed. 'I see. If Nico and I could look it over on our own...'

I felt a sense of excitement when I heard those words. We had another mystery to solve at last, not a small one like I'd wished for, but a proper one. A girl gone missing!

'Very well,' said Zoe. 'I shall wait for you in the house.'

Thrax stepped into the shed, leaving me at the door. The place was so small there wasn't enough room for the both of us at the same time.

Bright morning light streamed in through a small square window. It had a lamp on the sill. There was straw on the floor, which smelt fresh and clean. A cot sat against one wall, with no headboard but an enormous soft-looking pillow. A small wooden chest stood beside it, with a crudely made perfume jar on it.

Thrax lifted the pillow off the bed and squeezed it in case there was something hidden in it. He peeled off a goatskin blanket and checked under the bed. Then he looked inside the wooden chest. When he was done, he started shifting the straw on the floor with his feet.

'What are you looking for?' I asked. 'A hidden trapdoor?'

Thrax didn't reply. He never does if you ask a silly question with an obvious answer. Smoothing down the straw, he lay on the bed and studied the walls.

'It is my theory, Nico,' he said, 'that people always hide valuable things in a place where they can keep a constant eye on them, even when they are in bed.'

He hummed to himself for a few moments, then sprang up. 'Aha!' He went to the wall across the room and peered closely at the bricks. 'Do you have a knife on you?'

'You know I don't carry knives.'

'Your broken reed pen, then. The one you use for cleaning your nails. It's in your bag, I believe.'

I handed him the pen. Now that I was looking closely, I noticed that one of the bricks in the wall had a hairline crack around it. It was loose. Thrax wedged the blunt end of the reed pen under it and prised it out.

A dark hole appeared as the brick came out. Thrax put in his hand and drew out two little cotton bags. One was filled with loose coins. The second one held a small amulet, a bracelet made of pierced stones strung on a piece of leather. Every pebble had a strange symbol painted on it.

Thrax put the amulet back in its bag and we returned it to its hiding place with the money.

'No word about the money and the amulet to Zoe or her mother,' he whispered as we headed back to the farmhouse. Zoe had been busy while we were in the shed. She had filled the goatskins with wine and water and wrapped a warm dish in a piece of cotton. Her mother was tucked up in one of the cots and her soft snoring filled the room.

'I'll let her sleep till Father comes back home,' said Zoe, handing us the warm dish and another bag with bread and cheese. 'She's had a dreadful fright.'

'Tell her we said goodbye when she wakes up,' said Thrax. 'And please don't worry too much about your sister. I'm sure Nico and I will find her.'

Zoe nodded and kissed the tips of her fingers. 'May the gods listen to your words.'

'You must come and tell us at once if you have any news,' said Thrax. 'Meanwhile, Nico and I will start our investigations right away.'

We nodded our goodbyes and walked back up the dirt track, weighed down with food and wine. The full goatskin was surprisingly heavy on my back. 'It's going to be very difficult finding this girl,' I said, puffing in the morning heat. 'You didn't even ask Zoe for a description of her.'

'I didn't need to,' said Thrax.

I stopped to shift the goatskin from one shoulder to another. 'Oh?'

'We know what the missing girl looks like already.'

'Do we?'

'That epiblema the farmer's wife had on her lap?' said Thrax. 'We've seen it somewhere before. The girl in the cheesemaker's yard was wearing it. That boy Belos and his friends tore it from her shoulder. Selene is the girl with the red hair.'

'Oh!'

'And she didn't run away. She was kidnapped.'

CHAPTER NINE

A New Investigation

'Kidnapped!' I gasped. 'What makes you think that?'

'The bags in the hidey-hole. The things in them were special enough for Selene to hide. If she had run away, she would have taken them with her.'

'Should we tell Zoe?' I asked.

'I think the family is upset enough as it is. We'll tell them after we've found Selene.'

'And here I was thinking nothing nasty ever happens in sacred places.'

Thrax chuckled. 'Sacred places have the most powerful communities in the world. They influence kings and generals. And where there's power, there's always foul play of some sort.'

'But *why* was Selene kidnapped?'

'We'll know that when we find her,' said Thrax.

'You seem very sure that we will.'

Thrax walked faster, his feet stamping on the rocky ground. 'Did you not see that mother crying? I can't leave a woman to grieve for her child if I can help it.'

I thought of Thrax's mother, who might be sitting at home even now, hoping and praying to the gods that her son would be returned to her.

'Where do we start our search?'

'At the agora,' replied Thrax. 'It's the heart of the community, especially in a small mountain place like Delphi where all the locals know each other. If we keep our eyes and ears open, we're bound to pick up some vital information.'

'Selene might have been carried away by mountain bandits,' I said.

Thrax switched the food dish from one arm to the other. 'Bandits wouldn't dare come so close to Delphi during the months the oracle is open, not since Athens sent a small army to deal with them.'

Sadly, we had no more time to discuss our investigation because we'd reached the country house. Master Ariston welcomed us with a furious scowl. 'What kept you?' he asked. 'I am about to pass out with hunger.'

'We're sorry, master,' said Thrax, hastily laying the table. 'The farmer and his family are very upset. They think their youngest daughter has run away.'

'That odd-looking girl with the flaming-red hair?' snorted Master Ariston. 'I saw her making honey cakes when I went to see the farmer. I saw her last night too, when I was coming home from my "thinking walk". She was scurrying along the mountain path after some boy.'

'What time was this?' said Thrax, setting out the food we had brought.

'Too late in the evening for a young girl to be out chasing boys,' said Master Ariston. 'The stars were in the sky.'

Thrax tore up the bread, dipped it in wine and placed it on the table. 'Zoe told us Selene had an argument with her father earlier that night. Did she look upset?'

'I didn't give the child a second glance. I only recognised her because of those enormous green eyes she has.'

'What about the boy?' asked Thrax. 'Did you get a good look at him?'

Master Ariston scowled at Thrax, his mouth full of half-chewed bread. 'I'm afraid I was too engrossed with my play to have noticed what the boy looked like. Nico, fetch your pens. We're so late starting today, we'll have to work extra hard to catch up.'

The morning dragged on and on, with Master Ariston making up one ridiculous piece of dialogue after another. If his comedy was ever to be performed, I pitied the poor actors who would have to act these lines, and the audience that would have to sit and listen to them. I found it very hard to concentrate too. My mind kept wandering to the new mystery we had to solve.

Who had kidnapped Selene? And why? And, most important of all, where was she now? Was she somewhere we could rescue her?

Late in the afternoon, Master Ariston yawned and scratched his armpits. He asked Thrax to heat up the dish that Zoe had given us. It was sausage stew, and he wolfed it down without leaving any for Thrax and me.

'My imagination has run dry,' he said. 'Let's take the rest of the day off. I'll go to the baths for a soak and a think.'

'May Thrax and I go and buy petasos at the agora, sir?' I asked. 'We've both lost our old ones.'

'As long as you use your own money,' replied Master Ariston. 'And get me some dried chickpeas while you're there. Use your own money for that too, seeing as you have enough to splash out on new sun hats. Thrax can roast them for snacks.'

It was exciting leaving the country house that day. We couldn't wait to start our enquiries. Thrax and I both tried not to look too eager as we hurried down the lane, leaving Master Ariston to gather his own things for his trip to the baths.

CHAPTER TEN

The Blind Man with the Aulos

'This is what we have so far,' said Thrax as we walked into Delphi. 'Selene had a furious argument with her father yesterday just before sundown. Later, when the stars were out, she slipped out of her house to meet someone, a boy. Some time after that she was kidnapped. She hasn't been seen since.'

'I wonder who that mysterious boy was,' I said. 'He might have been the kidnapper.'

'Possibly. Or possibly not,' replied Thrax. 'Selene could have disappeared any time between then and the morning when Zoe found the shed empty.'

We came to the agora. 'Remember,' warned Thrax, 'we are here to buy sun hats and chickpeas. No talk of Selene or kidnappers. We are visitors and must not look or sound interested in local matters or we'll make people suspicious. You can bet that the kidnapper will have his ear to the ground until the fuss dies down.'

The marketplace was busy despite the lack of pilgrims. This being Delphi, there were lots of people selling holy objects to do with the oracle: small statues of Apollo, oil lamps, and strange round stones wrapped in miniature woollen nets.

'Those are called omphalos,' explained one of the stallholders when he saw us inspecting them. 'They represent navels, because we believe Delphi is the centre – the belly button – of the world. These are small copies of the original omphalos in the oracle, and they're going cheap today…'

'We're only looking, thanks,' said Thrax hurriedly. 'My master sent us to buy chickpeas for roasting.'

'We'll not get any information out of him,' he said, as we walked away.

'Why not?'

'Did you not get a good look at his clothes? His chiton is spotless and his belt is a very expensive one. He's a very successful trader. People like that are too guarded to gossip. They leave their talk for the andron and the symposium where only other rich men can hear. We need to eavesdrop on the fishmongers and the vegetable sellers. Ordinary folk who never get invited to symposiums. They're the ones who notice things and don't mind sharing them, mainly because gossip is the only entertainment they can afford.'

We made our way across the market to where people were selling fresh produce. The smell of fish was overpowering but it did not seem to prevent customers from lingering at the stall for a good old chat. Thrax stopped by a stall, pretending to admire the fish. His instincts are always accurate and within moments, we overheard someone talking about Selene.

'Poor Harmonia and Heliodorus,' said an old woman so bent with age she seemed to be looking at the ground while she talked. 'Their daughter Selene has run away.'

'That girl is a strange one,' said the vendor, wrapping anchovies in a filthy piece of cloth and putting them in the old woman's basket. 'Wouldn't surprise me if she's just hiding in some cave or disused farm to scare her parents. They'll find her soon, no doubt.'

The old woman counted out coins into the fishmonger's hand. 'May the gods bring the girl back home safely.'

Thrax nudged me. 'Nico, buy us some food, will you, please? I'm starving.'

I dug in my money bag and stopped a street seller who was selling fried fish wrapped in flatbread.

'Let's go and eat somewhere quiet,' I said.

'No,' said Thrax. 'We're staying here.'

He indicated a patch of ground where an old beggar with a crown of white hair was squatting, a small bowl at his right knee. He had very wrinkled skin and his eyes were a milky yellow. The man had been playing an aulos but had stopped when the old woman started talking, his head cocked to one side as he listened. Thrax dropped on the ground next to him and thrust half his snack into his hands.

'Share our good fortune with us, sir.'

'The gods bless you,' said the aulos player, sniffing at the food before taking a bite.

Thrax nodded at me to sit next to him. 'That's a nicely carved flute, sir,' he said.

'I whittled it myself up in the mountains,' said the old beggar. 'A long time ago when I could still see. It has been a very faithful companion. Her and old Aphrodite, my dog. Aphrodite is long gone now. Only the aulos remains.'

Thrax chewed his bread. 'You play it well. I love goatherd music. It's sad and playful at the same time.'

The old beggar seemed delighted by Thrax's words. 'My name is Tros. You have heard goatherd music often, then?'

'I grew up in the country,' said Thrax.

'I would still be up on the mountain if it were not for my eyes,' said Tros. 'But the ground gets too slippery with snow and frost and the mountain air is too harsh on my aging bones.'

'It must have been lonely being a goatherd, with only a flute and your dog for company,' said Thrax.

The beggar smiled wistfully. 'Ah, but I had many friends on the mountain. Other goatherds, and hunters who came in search of wild boar and deer. And the caves were full of people too. Those who can afford it come to Delphi to seek the advice of Apollo the sun god. But in the winter months others climb up to the caves to consult Pan or worship Dionysus and the earth goddess.'

Tros gazed up at Mount Parnassus with his sightless eyes.

'You mean there is a second oracle on Mount Parnassus?' I asked.

'If you follow the path that goes past the missing girl's house, you will come to a cave high up in the mountain. Sacred water drips through its roof, filling it with the power of the gods. The priests call it the Corcyian cave. We know it as the cave of shadows. There are women there who can tell you your future or make you a powerful charm for a few obols. They consult the earth goddess through the knucklebones or the stones.'

Tros finished the snack and wiped his hands on his dirty chiton. 'This red-haired girl who ran away. She too can read the knucklebones. The goatherds say she is very talented. The earth goddess has given her much power. In time, she will be even more respected than her mentor.'

'The girl has a mentor?' said Thrax.

Tros nodded and smiled, showing the stumpy remains of brown teeth.

From the corner of my eye, I spotted Belos buying fried fish from the wandering seller. I hoped he wouldn't spot us. The idea of another fight with his gang filled me with dread.

'What's the mentor's name, do you know?' asked Thrax, taking a coin out of my purse and dropping it in Tros's bowl.

'No one knows her real name,' answered the old man as he raised the aulos to his lips. 'But her followers call her Mother Kessandra. You will find her in the Corcyian cave.'

CHAPTER ELEVEN

Mother Kessandra

Tros's eerie mountain music followed us as we left the agora with our new petasos and a huge bag of chickpeas for Master Ariston.

'Did you see Belos?' I asked. 'He was buying food from the street seller.'

'Yes, I saw him,' said Thrax. 'He's obviously a baker's apprentice.'

'How did you figure that out?'

'He had flour up to his elbows.'

I hadn't even seen Thrax turn his head to look at Belos, so I had no idea how he'd noticed the flour on Belos's arms.

'We must go and see Mother Kessandra in the Corcyian cave,' he said. 'Selene might have told her something that will give us a clue.'

Visiting Mother Kessandra, however, turned out to be quite a challenge. Master Ariston was so busy with his play, I didn't have time to even leave the house for three whole days, let alone go up the mountain. Looking out of the window as I worked, I could see Thrax busy with the hives, lifting out honeycombs and scraping the honey into pots. My tummy rumbled with hunger at the sight of them. How I wished I could be out in the open air too, with the spring sun on my back.

That sun didn't last for long, though. When, at last, Master Ariston decided we should take a day off, the heavens opened and it rained for the next ten days without stopping. There was so much water cascading down the mountain, the country house was in danger of being swept along with it. The orchard was flooded and we had to sleep indoors.

Zoe braved the wild weather every day to make sure we were still in one piece and to bring more supplies. She had no more information about Selene to give us. No one had seen her.

The gods favoured us when at last the rains stopped and Master Ariston ventured out to the baths. He came back with a big grin on his face. 'One of the local merchants has invited me and Gorgias to join him on a trip to Kirrha tomorrow. He is buying carpets. I might buy one for Mother.'

The journey to Kirrha and back can be done in a day, with time for shopping and lunch at an inn if one sets off before dawn. Here at last was the perfect opportunity to visit Mother Kessandra.

We left the country house the moment Master Ariston disappeared down the mountain on Ariana. We took bread and some honey cakes with us but no water; with so much rain, we knew the mountain springs would be overflowing.

The road to the Corcyian cave was much longer than we expected, following a steep mountain path that became narrower and narrower as we climbed. The only sound was that of burbling water; the streams were indeed full to overflowing after the recent storms. The ground was often muddy and I had to be careful not to slip.

We entered a dark wood where a small shrine to the nymphs overlooked a spring. We stopped to drink, the water icy on our hands and lips. Refreshed, we moved on and at last the path widened, leading to a small plateau backed with a cliff. It was clear of trees and the entrance to a dark cave loomed before us, an ancient altar standing right in the middle of it.

'This must be it,' said Thrax. 'The famous Corcyian cave.'

'The cave of shadows.'

We made our way past the altar into darkness as solid as rock. We could hear the sound of dripping water, and the distant hum of people praying.

As our eyes got used to the dark, we could see that the cave stretched into the distance. There were great big pools of water all around us, which caught water dripping from the ceiling. They reflected the shiny blackness of the walls.

In the distance, in what seemed like a doorway to a second cave, a fire was burning. People were sitting around it, stiff and immobile as if in a trance. They were the ones making the humming sound. We walked towards them.

As we got closer, the people stirred and crept away into the darkness, leaving just one figure in the light. A small woman, thin as a spear, with wild black hair and a shawl around her shoulders. Her eyes were closed and the flickering light that rippled across her withered face made her look frightening, like Medusa. A strange snoring sound came from her throat.

All at once, the woman's eyes snapped open, making me jump, and she spoke in a hoarse whisper.

'You come to seek the advice of the stones?'

'We are looking for Mother Kessandra,' replied Thrax. He nodded at me and I placed the honey cakes at her side as a gift.

The woman held a hand to her withered chest. 'This is Mother Kessandra.'

'We need information about a girl,' said Thrax. 'Selene, the farmer's daughter.'

The woman's eyes flickered at the mention of Selene's name. 'Who seeks this knowledge?'

'We are new friends of her family,' answered Thrax. 'Selene has disappeared.'

Mother Kessandra's face twitched but she said nothing.

'Her mother has begged us to find her,' Thrax volunteered.

Very slowly, Mother Kessandra held out a cup and rattled it. 'Pick one stone each.'

Thrax and I both drew a pebble.

'Hold them up to the fire. Let me see them.'

We opened our hands to show her.

'A red for the well-built child,' whispered Mother Kessandra. 'The courage is strong within you.' She peered at my stone. 'Green for the well fed one. You are a child of kindness.'

She took both pebbles and pressed them to her forehead. 'The power of the stones assures me you are to be trusted. I shall speak. Selene came to see me about a nightmare that keeps her awake at night. A bad dream where she is being pursued by a man riding a monstrous turtle. He chases her along a raging river, where the water and the darkness threaten to swallow her up. He drives her right over the edge of a precipice, into a bottomless void. Her dream ends there. She wakes up without knowing if she is to drown or to live.'

'How long ago was this?' asked Thrax.

'Winter. The mountains were still covered in snow.'

'I believe Selene was kidnapped,' said Thrax. 'Could the man on the turtle be the kidnapper?'

Mother Kessandra shook her little clay cup and the pebbles tumbled out close to the fire. She inspected them for a long while, her fingers rippling over them. 'The stones have not fallen in the pattern I seek. The goddess refuses to speak.'

She brushed the pebbles aside and looked from Thrax to me. 'Continue to seek my pupil, I beg you. But beware! Both of you are in mortal danger.'

CHAPTER TWELVE

Ambush!

'That was all very dramatic,' I said as we left the cave. 'And I have to admit, quite scary too.'

'It was meant to be,' said Thrax. 'That's how oracles operate, by scaring you into believing them. But even if she is a fake, old Mother Kessandra did give us a very good clue. The man riding the monstrous turtle.'

'Surely we can't base our investigations on a dream?'

'I once heard someone talk about dreams at a symposium. He mentioned a famous philosopher who lived long ago. His name was Thales of Miletus and he believed that things in our lives are not determined by the gods as we believe. They are determined by us mortals and our actions. I do not believe dreams come from the rulers of Mount Olympus. They come from somewhere deep within us, from an unknown part of ourselves. They are sent to guide us and to alert us to danger.'

'So are you saying that Selene was warned in a dream that she would be kidnapped by a man on a turtle – and her dream came true?'

'I don't think the kidnapper was actually riding a turtle,' said Thrax. 'Perhaps that's how Selene saw him in her dreams. But in some way the kidnapper has a connection with turtles.'

'We saw Milo actually riding a turtle,' I gasped. 'But surely he can't be a kidnapper. He wouldn't harm a fly, let alone a child.'

'Ha, there's more to Milo than meets the eye,' said Thrax.

'What makes you say that?'

'Those bruises on his face for a start,' said Thrax. 'It looked to me like he had been in a fight.'

'I thought he might have slipped on the shore and banged his face, or fallen off his horse.'

'Those bruises were made by a fist. You could actually make out the outlines of the knuckles.'

The steep path from the cave of shadows started to level out and we entered the wood. Suddenly a blood-curdling roar made me jump. On either side of us, dark figures leaped out of the bushes. We were surrounded by a gang wielding cudgels.

Thrax, his muscled clenched, swooped at the ground and came back up with a thick fallen branch. He smashed it in two across his thigh and handed one half to me.

'Stay close, Nico.'

I tried to say yes but no sound came out of my mouth. My voice always lets me down when I'm terrified. Our attackers, their himations pulled over their heads, closed in on us. Thrax leaped at them. I heard him grunt as he lashed out with the cudgel and several of our assailants fell back, blood soaking their himations.

I tried to raise my own cudgel but it was snatched from me in an instant. Someone kicked my feet out from under me and sent me reeling to the ground. I lay in the dirt, my body shaking with pain and my face burning with shame.

Why couldn't I ever help Thrax when he needed me?

Somehow that shaming thought gave me courage. I screamed and leaped back to my feet. A moment later my teeth were clamped firmly on a fleshy arm close to me. My victim roared with pain and I saw the fist on his other arm rushing at my face. It wasn't fast enough. A knock from Thrax's stick sent the boy sprawling into the bushes.

'Well done, Nico,' he said. 'That's another one down.'

Just then a piercing whistle sounded and goatherds started jumping down from the trees. They fell on the assailants, hitting out with their rounded crooks. I have no idea how long the fight lasted but when it was over there were no dark figures left. They had all dragged themselves back into the woods.

'We stand in your debt,' said Thrax, throwing away the cudgel. He had a new black eye and bruises on both his arms. I myself had a cut on my right knee and I could feel a burning pain spreading across my back.

'Old Tros asked us to look out for you,' said the goatherd. 'He's my great uncle.'

'We must go to the agora and thank him,' I said, trying to brush the dirt from my chiton. 'You helped us survive our first encounter with mountain bandits.'

'Those hoodlums weren't mountain bandits,' said Thrax. 'Mountain bandits don't roar before they attack. They lie in wait to ambush you. Anyway, bandits haven't been able to get to Mount Parnassus for a while. There was a massive rockfall in the winter and the mountain pass is blocked. It will take months to clear it. We were attacked by kids from the city.'

Kids from the city! Perhaps they were the gang we met on our first night, trying to get their promised revenge. Or did someone know we were looking for Selene?

The goatherds saw us to the edge of the wood and we continued down the mountain. I tried not to wince at the pain as I hobbled on my injured leg. Mother Kessandra's warning had come true a bit too quickly for my liking. This was turning out to be quite a dangerous adventure.

CHAPTER THIRTEEN

Milo's Secret Meeting

'Not again,' cried Master Ariston when he saw our new injuries. 'You two are turning into proper cuthroats.'

His face was pale and he was shaking all over. The trip to Kirrha had been very enjoyable but Master Ariston had come back with his guts on fire.

'Never ever eat shellfish in a harbour town, boys,' he groaned, clutching his belly. 'Your master is poisoned. I do not expect to see the sunrise.'

Thrax and I got him into bed. I cooled his forehead with a wet rag while Thrax made him a drink of hot water and mint to settle his stomach. Once he was asleep, we left a large chamber pot by his bed just in case and climbed up into the tree house.

I took out my wax tablet and made some notes, clutching the Medusa League medallion at my neck. So much in this case was happening so quickly, I wanted to make sure I wouldn't forget anything.

'Nico,' Thrax said from his cot, 'I know you think Milo is too gentle a man to be a kidnapper but he is the only suspect we have at the moment. Let's tail him and see what happens.'

'We'll start tomorrow if we can,' I said, putting the wax tablet on its special shelf. 'And let's hope we don't get attacked again. Goodnight, Thrax.'

'Goodnight.'

We got up before dawn to find Master Ariston still too weak to get out of bed. Thrax made him more hot water and mint, cleaned his face and arms with a wet rag, and emptied the chamber pot in the garden.

'Nico and I are going out, master,' he said. 'We've left a note for Zoe to make you some more medicine when she arrives. Don't be tempted to eat any rich food or it'll take you longer to get better.'

Master Ariston was too sick to argue. I felt bad about leaving him alone when he might need our help, but it must have been the gods themselves urging us on with our investigation. That day we were to discover the most important clue in our case.

As far as we knew, Gorgias and Milo were still lodging in the centre of Delphi. We made our way there, both pulling up our himations over our heads.

'There's a tavern across the road from the inn,' said Thrax. 'Order us something to drink, Nico. If someone asks, we're waiting for our master.'

We didn't have to wait long before we saw Gorgias trotting out of the inn on his horse. Solon followed on a donkey. The innkeeper came rushing out after them, a white cleaning rag flapping in his hand.

'Will you be wanting lunch, sir?'

'No, I am dining with friends.'

Not long afterwards Milo left the inn on foot. He was frowning and his chiton, normally pristine, was all crumpled. The innkeeper bustled out behind him.

'Will you be wanting lunch, sir? We have a stew of wild onions especially for you.'

Milo ignored him and walked on. Thrax and I waited until he was halfway down the street, then tucked our belts around our chitons and followed him. He led us to a large commercial stable on the outskirts of Delphi, where he banged the doorknocker and was let in. When he came out again, he was riding a black horse.

'How odd,' I said. 'Milo has his own horse. Why is he using a different one?'

'He doesn't want anyone to know he's going for a ride,' said Thrax. 'I think he's leaving Delphi. Wait here for me, Nico.'

He knocked on the stable door and was let in too. A few moments later he came out, holding the reins of a chestnut-coloured horse.

'How did you pay for that?' I gasped.

He laughed. 'Not an obol. Stables always have at least one horse who's too skittish for most people to ride. I offered to borrow this one to help break her in. Her name is Rhea.'

'But how did you get the stable master to trust you?'

'The stable master is an aging woman,' said Thrax. 'I used my boyish charms. Now hurry up before she changes her mind.'

He helped me up on to Rhea's glossy back and we trotted down the street. I was afraid the beast might suddenly rear up and throw us off but, under Thrax's spell, she was as docile as a dove.

We joined a steady stream of people leaving Delphi, mostly farmers in carts who were delivering produce to Kirrha. Up ahead, Milo's black horse galloped at quite a pace and we followed him down the mountain to the plain.

Soon, Milo came to a dust-ridden altar and turned off the main road. We saw him disappear down a dirt track between two ancient fig trees. Thrax pulled on the reins to slow Rhea down.

'Whoa, girl.'

We waited for a while, then turned on to the dirt track ourselves. It was lined with fig trees, their branches meeting overhead to form a tunnel. They were so low, we had to bend to avoid them. After the noise and bustle of the main road, it was strangely silent in the tunnel. It was strangely silent, like being in a graveyard.

The tunnel gave out on to abandoned farmland. Before us lay the remains of a farmhouse, the orchard around it choked with tall weeds and bushes. The only building standing was a disused barn with dirty walls. We were looking at its back. There were no doors or windows but loud voices echoed from its collapsed roof.

'Can you hear that?' whispered Thrax as he tied Rhea out of sight behind an overgrown pomegranate tree. 'Come on, let's get closer.'

He crouched down in the tall weeds and I crawled after him towards the barn. Coming round the corner we could see more tumbledown buildings. One of them had an altar outside the remains of a door. A headless statue of a god stood on it. Three horses were tied to a post nearby, nibbling on the grass. One of them was Milo's.

The voices in the barn grew louder and angrier.

'I said, is this all you have?'

A trembling high-pitched voice answered. 'It's all I could get at short notice.'

I recognised that voice at once. It was Milo.

'We followed you all the way from New Sybaris for a handful of coins? There's not enough here to keep my horse in hay for a day.'

'I don't know why you had to follow me here,' argued Milo. 'I told you I'd pay in full when I got back home.'

'We fancied a trip to Kirrha,' growled another voice. 'Though it's turned out to be an even dirtier dung heap than New Sybaris. If you don't give us something to impress the boss soon, we might have to come and talk to your papa in Delphi.'

'Please,' said Milo. 'Give me some more time. I beg you.'

'People like you always want more time,' growled the first voice. 'But you just keep on gambling and losing more money. The boss is running out of patience.'

'Yes,' cut in someone else, his voice sharp with menace. 'And the interest on your debt is growing by the day. You only brought something worth more than a few obols once.'

'That should have paid off all my debts to you. It's a priceless thing,' groaned Milo. 'You're cheating.'

His words were cut short and he cried out. Someone must have punched him in the stomach. 'Remember, rich boy,' we're always on your trail. There's no escaping us.'

There was a burst of cruel laughter, then the door creaked open and the rough men came out. One of them kicked the headless god off its altar. Then they got in their saddles and galloped right past us, their horses kicking up dust in our faces.

Milo staggered out just as I wiped my eyes clean. The poor man was clutching his stomach. He looked absolutely terrified.

CHAPTER FOURTEEN

The Boy in the Himation

We came home to find Master Ariston feeling much better. Zoe had stopped by and mixed him a strong potion of honey and figs that cleared his stomach at once. He was so happy he did not even ask where we'd been all day.

'She left sausages for you two,' he said, scratching away at his tablet. 'Please eat them outside and keep your voices low. Make sure you get a good night's sleep, Nico. We have a lot of work ahead of us tomorrow.'

We stoked the fire in the cracked hydria and climbed up to our tree house to eat. I knew Thrax was thinking hard because he would hardly say a word. I wasn't in the mood for talking either. The sight of poor Milo staggering out of that barn had left me shaken.

The moon came out and bats flitted above our tree. The beehives were silent. High on the mountain I heard the distant howling of a wolf. The lonely sound made me think of my parents in Kos. I must go and see them soon. Perhaps I could take them a small omphalos from Delphi. My mother especially would like that.

Thrax sat up in his cot without warning. 'Eureka! I have figured it out, Nico. The whole thing.'

I sat up too, making my branch of the olive tree sway dangerously. 'Have you? You know who kidnapped Selene and why? It's not Milo, is it?'

'No,' said Thrax. 'You were right. It's not Milo. It's someone else. And he had an accomplice.'

'Do you mean there are two kidnappers?'

'Yes! That's why I found it so difficult to work out what happened. I was expecting there to be only one.'

'Who are they?'

'I have a few details to clear up first,' said Thrax. 'And then I'll tell you.'

'That's not fair...' I began to argue.

But Thrax cut me short. 'Nico, we need to get out of this tree. We're in danger!'

'Danger?' I said, clambering down the tree after him. 'From whom? The kidnappers? They're coming here?'

Thrax did not reply but pointed to the cracked hydria. Its flames threw light on the ground around it and I noticed footprints in the dust.

'Someone was snooping around the orchard while we were away,' said Thrax.

'Master Ariston could have made those footprints,' I said.

'No, his feet are bigger than this. Besides, I've seen these footprints before.'

'Where?'

'On the mountain pass coming down from the Corcyian cave the day we were attacked. One of those city boys has been here, and I think he'll return soon. Tonight!'

I looked around in alarm, half expecting a hooded figure to jump out from the dark. 'What do we do now?'

'We outwit him, Nico,' said Thrax. He ran to the barn and returned with an enormous bundle of straw. He divided it in two and we carried it up into the tree. Following Thrax's lead, I tucked my half into my cot, smoothing down the himation around it to make it look like a sleeping body.

Next, we fetched a full goatskin and hid it behind a nearby bush. Then we went indoors and Thrax shook Master Ariston awake.

'What's happening?' Master Ariston gasped, his bleary eyes looking from Thrax to me.

'We need your help, master,' said Thrax. 'Will you come to the window?'

'To the window? Now?'

'Yes, our lives might be in danger.'

'Danger?' mumbled Master Ariston. The word didn't seem to have much effect on him but he let

Thrax lead him to the window, which looked out on the orchard.

'What am I meant to be looking at?'

'We're expecting an uninvited guest,' said Thrax, pulling up a stool for Master Ariston to sit on. 'He'll be up to no good. We need you as a witness, master. Sit here.'

'A witness,' mumbled Master Ariston, looking even more confused.

'That's right,' said Thrax. 'An upstanding member of the community that a magistrate like your friend Glykon would believe.'

Master Ariston gawped. 'I don't know what game you're playing, my boy, but if it's an upstanding member of the community you need...' His head sagged on to his chest before he could finish the sentence. He started snoring.

'Let him snooze,' said Thrax. 'I'm going out to the orchard. Wake him up when you see the intruder.'

I didn't have to wait long before a dark shadow appeared in the orchard, peering around. For a moment it looked directly at the open window, sending me stumbling back into the shadows. I watched breathless as the intruder approached the olive tree, its black himation shimmering like the dark pools in the Corcyian cave.

I shook Master Ariston awake.

'Ha...?'

Under the tree, the mysterious figure pulled a flask from the folds of its himation. I smelt the aroma of olive oil as it sprinkled the contents around the roots. The intruder flung the empty flask away, then kicked over the smouldering hydria, scattering the glowing embers. The dry weeds under the tree caught fire at once.

It took only moments for the tree itself to burst into flames, lighting up the orchard with a horrific glow.

'Master,' I called helplessly.

But Mister Ariston had already leapt off the stool, all traces of sleepiness gone. He let out a blood-curdling yell. 'Someone, grab that man. He is an arsonist.'

I saw Thrax leap out from his hiding place and whip the intruder's himation off his head. The arsonist's face was revealed.

It was Belos!

CHAPTER FIFTEEN

A Deal with Belos

'Good morning,' said Thrax cheerfully. 'How are you feeling today, Belos?'

After Thrax unmasked the baker's apprentice, the boy had fled from the orchard. But it had been easy to track him down to the bakery. It seemed Belos was well known in Delphi. All we had to do was ask for him at the agora, which was full of slaves waiting to buy food for their masters' breakfast.

He looked at us defiantly from behind a wooden table, his arms buried up to the elbows in dough. 'What do you want?'

'We want to make a deal.'

Belos snorted in derision, brown flour coming off his face in a cloud. 'What kind of deal?'

'We'll pretend you never set fire to our house—'

'It's not your house,' said Belos. 'You're only renting.'

'Destroying people's property is still a crime, whoever is living in it. Not to mention endangering people's lives. I would say that's attempted murder. What were you trying to do, Belos? Scare us into ending our investigation? Yesterday was your second attempt, wasn't it? The first was on the mountain path, coming down from the Corcyian cave.

'I have to say you're very clever. You started tailing us after our little fight outside the cheesemaker's, looking for a way to get your promised revenge. And after Selene's disappearance you discovered we were looking for her. You learned we were friendly with Zoe, her sister. You saw us talking to Tros at the agora. How did you find out he'd given us information about Mother Kessandra? Did you ask nicely or did you threaten him with violence?'

'As a matter of fact, I just eavesdropped on your conversation,' sneered Belos. 'Call yourself clever. I could hear every word you said to the blind man from a market stall nearby. Anyway, you have no proof it was me who attacked you, either on the mountain or in the orchard.'

'Our master was watching at the window. If we reported the crime to Glykon the magistrate, he might not believe a lowly slave or a scribe, but Master Ariston is a respected elder. His words carry weight.'

Belos scoffed, his rough hands still kneading the dough. 'Your master was fast asleep. I could hear him snoring.'

'Master Ariston woke up in time to see you,' said Thrax. 'He not only saw you setting fire to the olive tree, he saw me do something else too.'

Belos's eyes flickered. 'What?'

Thrax reached under his belt and pulled out something, which he held in his closed fist. 'When I leaped on you,' he said to Belos, 'I didn't just yank the himation down from your head. I also snatched this from your chiton.' He opened his hand. In it was a golden fibula shaped like a man riding a turtle.

'I'd say this is proof that you were the arsonist in the orchard. All I need to do is find just one person who is willing to admit they have seen you wearing this. One of your money-hungry friends, perhaps.'

Belos jerked his hands out of the dough. 'Give that back.'

'It's a very expensive thing for a baker's apprentice to have,' said Thrax, closing his hand around the fibula. 'And quite a rare design too. I caught a flash of it inside your himation during our scrap in the cheesemaker's yard and thought how odd it was that someone should hide such a beautiful fibula instead of showing it off. I'd say it was made in Aegina, the island of the turtles. Same as the coins that fell out of your money bag. They had turtles on them too. The priest Abantes gave you the coins and the fibula, didn't he? Or perhaps you stole them from him.'

'Why would Abantes give me money and presents?' growled Belos, chewing on his lower lip in frustration. 'I've never spoken to the priest. I don't even know him.'

'Oh, but you do,' said Thrax. 'Although you try to keep your connection a secret. Abantes is your father.'

Belos's face went bright red at the revelation. 'Abantes? My father? Where's the proof of that, slave?'

'I am looking at it right now,' said Thrax. 'You chew your lower lip when you are lying, just like your father. I believe Abantes met your mother when he visited Delphi fourteen years ago and you were the result. Only he couldn't tell anyone he had a son. He was married at the time and being unfaithful to your wife is a crime. It's only when his wife died that he could come back to Delphi, to find you.'

'You have no proof,' spat Belos again but this time his words did not sound so convincing.

'We have proof that you set fire to our olive tree. That alone is enough to land you in trouble with the law. I wonder what the punishment for arson is. I'd say exile at the very least. Perhaps they might throw you off a cliff like they did with Aesop the storyteller a long time ago. I believe he was accused of stealing a silver cup from the temple.'

Belos's face turned a bright red. 'So what's the deal?'

'Take us to Selene,' said Thrax. 'I think you and Abantes have hidden her up the mountain, while you wait for bandits to take her away and sell her into slavery.'

'Ha,' cried Belos, 'as if I could make that gorgon go anywhere with me.'

'Oh, but you lured her up there. You bribed one of your unscrupulous friends to go to her with a false message. He told her that Mother Kessandra wanted to speak to her urgently in the cave of shadows. Master Ariston saw her following your minion the night she disappeared. And when he delivered her to you, you and your father dragged her off to a secret hiding place. Only the bandits haven't come for her yet, have they? There was a huge rockfall in the mountain pass, which will take months to clear. Bet you and your father didn't know about that.'

Belos opened and shut his mouth like a fish and his puffy cheeks quivered. He was trying to speak but no words came out.

'Kidnapping, arson, your list of crimes keeps on growing,' said Thrax. 'Do we have a deal? You take us to Selene, and we'll promise not to go to the magistrate.'

Belos nodded angrily. 'All right. But I want my fibula back.'

'All in good time,' said Thrax, returning the golden pin to the folds of his own chiton. 'We should leave now, before the master baker arrives and asks where his apprentice is going.'

I was full of admiration for Thrax as we hurried along the streets of Delphi. Only a person with his intelligence and logical thinking could recognise random clues and put them together as he had. But there was one question that still puzzled me. Why on earth should Abantes and Belos want to kidnap Selene?

CHAPTER SIXTEEN

The Forgotten City

We left Delphi as the rising sun was starting to melt away the morning mist, taking the mountain pass that led up to the Corcyian cave. The ground was still sodden and slippery from the recent rains, and I regretted not wearing my boots, which had firmer soles than my sandals.

Sadly, there was no time to go back home and fetch them. Master Ariston would be wide awake by now and wondering where Thrax and

I had gone. I sent a quick prayer to Apollo and the muses that he would not be too angry with us when we returned.

We passed a few goatherds who gave Thrax and me a cheery nod. Belos had pulled his himation up around his face and the goatherds did not recognise him. He walked in sullen silence, lost in his own thoughts.

Further up the mountain, the morning mist still drifted among the windblown trees and thorny bushes. We stopped to drink from the spring, then entered the wood where we'd been attacked two days earlier.

As we passed the cave and continued up the mountain, I could feel a difference in the air. Below, the world was tamed, the land turned to fields, orchards and dwellings. It was the world of our much-loved gods, Apollo and Pan and Dionysus. The world of our Hellenic culture. Up here, the world felt wild and untamed. A place where the powerful beings that had been there before Zeus and the Olympians still ruled. Everything seemed ancient. The rocks were worn smooth by the wind or covered in faded yellow lichen. The stunted trees reached out with gnarled, knotted branches.

The path grew stonier and narrower, snaking round boulders and prickly bushes. The only signs of life were the vultures soaring overhead and small clusters of spring flowers growing out of cracks in the rocks.

I had never before walked so far without stopping. My knees started to hurt and my feet swelled like sponges dipped in water. The straps on my sandals cut into my ankles.

'Take them off,' said Thrax, who was already barefoot. 'Your feet will thank you for it.'

I did as he said, putting the sandals in my bag. The thin mountain air was making me light-headed and I shivered despite the blinding sunshine.

The path followed the curve round the mountain away from Delphi. Now all I could see below was a wild valley full of trees and the odd wisp of smoke rising from a farmhouse kitchen.

We came to a narrow tunnel. Belos urged us on with a grunt. We followed him and came out on to a small plateau. Before us lay the ruins of what looked like an ancient wall, circling the remains of long-fallen buildings. Thrax and I stared wide-eyed in amazement.

We had stumbled on a small long-lost city.

CHAPTER SEVENTEEN
Legend and Reality

B elos pulled back his himation. 'Ha,' he said, enjoying the look in our eyes. 'Your master thinks he is so important, coming to ask Apollo's advice, showing off his wealth. But there were people on this mountain a long time before your precious oracle was even built. My mother's ancestors came to live here at the time of the Great Flood.'

He indicated the ruins around us. 'Nobody even remembers this place. Every year, the elements wear away more of these stones. Mount

Parnassus is prone to earthquakes. One day there will be no trace of the ancient peoples left, only the legends.'

'I know the old stories,' I gasped. A storyteller had once told them at a symposium Master Ariston performed in. 'One of them tells about the people who long ago lived at the foot of Mount Parnassus. They were alerted to the Great Flood you mention by the howling of wolves, who sensed the disaster coming. They fled up the mountain and founded a new city, which they called Lykoreia, in honour of the wolves.'

'Lykoreia,' said Belos, his lips trembling with the need to let the words out. 'It means the "howling of the wolves".'

'But surely that's just a legend,' said Thrax. 'An old story.'

'Who knows?' said Belos. 'It could be. Perhaps this city is older even than the legend.'

He started walking through the ruins, tracing his fingers along the stones. I looked around me with new eyes, imagining the wolves racing up the mountain to get away from the flood, terrified people following in their wake.

Had it really happened or was it just a story as Thrax insisted? Time draws a veil on events, turning the past into a dream nobody can remember clearly. Legend and reality mix. They become myth.

'Where have you hidden Selene?' Thrax asked Belos as we left the ruins behind and came once more to empty rocks.

Belos ignored him and hurried on. The plateau narrowed back to a mountain path and then to a dirt track so narrow we had to put one foot in front of the other to walk along it. To our right, the cliff was smooth as glass, with not even a crack in the rocks to cling to. To our left, it was a sheer drop to the valley below.

The sun was setting and it was difficult to see with all the shadows. Thrax reached out his left hand without turning. 'Hold on to me, Nico. We'll be fine.'

I took his hand and slowly, like snails crawling along a sodden leaf, we moved forward. My legs felt wobbly and my chest so tight I could hardly breathe.

Ahead of us, Belos stopped. He had come to a sort of platform jutting out over the valley below. Behind it was a small cave, its mouth bricked up with stones, leaving just enough space for a door. Belos pushed it open.

'Is Selene here?' Thrax said.

Belos nodded and we stepped inside. By the light from the door, I could make out an enormous rectangular stone in the middle of the cave. At first I thought it was an altar. Ancient peoples had been known to worship and offer sacrifice in caves. But this stone was too low to the ground for that and I noticed something lying on it. It was the crumbling remains of a skeleton. We were in a tomb.

My blood turned cold. I'd been in graveyards before, but never within touching distance of actual bones.

Belos ducked through a low doorway and we followed him down a narrow corridor cut into the rocks. It led to a small chamber where a lamp

was burning in an alcove. Belos held it up so we could see into the far corner. There, with both hands chained to the wall, was a girl. She was much thinner than the last time I had seen her and she was covered in dried mud. But there was no mistaking the red hair. It was Selene.

'You animal,' growled Thrax, turning round to face Belos. 'Look at her. She's practically dead.'

Alerted by the light, Selene rattled the chains feebly and moaned. Belos sniggered. 'The girl's still got some fight left in her. She's like a tiger. Grrr! But she's weak from lack of water. There's a flask just out of her reach if you want to help her, slave boy. Go on, the gods will reward you for your kindness.'

Thrax and I saw the flask at the same time, and we both jumped towards it without thinking. A moment later the ground opened up under our feet and we found ourselves hurtling into darkness.

CHAPTER EIGHTEEN

Buried Alive

We hit rocky ground and I felt a dizzying pain in my head. 'Ouch.'

'Are you hurt, Nico?'

'Not badly, Thrax but I'm seeing stars and I'm going to have a second lump on my head to match the first one. How about you?'

'I twisted my ankle but I think I'll live.'

'You'll live,' echoed a voice above us. 'But not for long.'

Belos was grinning down at us from the hole we'd fallen through, his face a hideous mask in the lamplight. 'You thought you had got the better of me but you have fallen for a trick that was old even in the days of the tomb robbers. Did you really think I would let you free Selene? I waited years for my father to find me. Nothing is going to take him away from me again.'

'We'll get out,' said Thrax. 'And we'll bring you to justice.'

'No, you won't,' spat Belos. 'You made a big mistake when you thought I'd brought that girl up here to wait for mountain bandits. I knew the mountain pass was blocked. No, I brought her here to die. Now you are going to perish with her. And when there's nothing left of you except bones, I shall come back and retrieve my fibula.'

He tossed some coins down to us. 'Use these to pay the ferryman for your journey across the Styx.' His face disappeared from the hole and we heard his boots trudging out of the chamber.

Without Belos's lamp, the darkness in the chamber was almost solid.

'The gods help us,' I whispered. 'What have we fallen into?'

'The chamber above us must have been a treasure house,' said Thrax. 'I have heard tell of ancient rulers who were buried with all their riches. That skeleton in the big cave is probably a dead king from long ago. We are in a trap meant to fool tomb robbers. Belos disguised it with twigs and sticks. I bet you the floor here is littered with the skulls and bones of dead thieves.'

Thrax shuffled closer to me. 'Nico, feel in your bag and tell me what's in it.'

I did as he asked. 'I have a stylus, two reed pens and a stale honey cake. Also a scrap of papyrus.'

'Where is your wax tablet?'

'It fell out of my belt and smashed on the floor.'

'Can you find it? I only need the wooden frame.'

I felt around in the dark, praying I would not accidentally touch a human bone.

'Good,' said Thrax when I found the broken tablet. 'I have Master Ariston's alabastron. It's nearly full of perfumed oil. Here, I'm setting it down on the floor between us. Don't knock it over. Now hand me your stylus and tear the papyrus to shreds. They need to be fine, like straw, and put them in a heap on the floor in front of you. Then tear a narrow strip off your chiton and stick it in the alabastron. Make sure the bottom half is hanging down in the oil and the top half is sticking out of the alabastron.'

I heard the sound of wood scraping against wood as I carried out his instructions. Thrax was grinding the sharp tip of the stylus against the wooden frame. There was a faint burning smell and eventually a small red ember glowed in the dark.

'Nico, the papyrus.'

I piled the shreds carefully around the ember and Thrax blew on them till a small flame appeared. We watched it blossom. Thrax picked up the alabastron and held the strip of chiton to the fire.

Now we had a lamp and we could see around us. The floor was indeed littered with bones. I could see a cracked skull grinning at me and a hand with bony fingers spread out on the ground.

'We need a stick or a branch,' said Thrax. 'A thick one that will take our weight.'

The pit was dug out of solid rock, with huge bumps and dents, and many hidden corners. We searched around and soon found the discarded handle of a broken axe.

Thrax took off his himation and tore it into strips, which he tied and twisted together to make a long rope. He knotted the end of it to the middle of the wooden handle and hurled it like a javelin through the hole in the roof. Twice it fell back into the pit but the third time, the two ends caught on the rim of the hole. Thrax tugged on it to make sure the rope was secure, then turned to me.

'You go first, Nico. I'll bring the lamp.'

I shimmied up the rope, grunting with the effort, the axe handle bending under my weight. Thrax came up behind me, grabbing the rope with one hand and holding the lamp in the other.

In the upper chamber, we both knelt down by Selene. She was so weak now, she could barely move. Her eyes were almost puffed shut.

'Can you hear me, Selene?' said Thrax. 'We're going to find a way to break your chains and get you out of here. We're friends and we've come to rescue you.'

Selene rattled her chains to show she understood. I held the water flask to her lips and she drank thirstily. Thrax gave her some honey cake.

With Selene fed, we looked around for the tunnel that led back to the ancient king's resting place. We found the entrance without a problem but the far end was blocked with a huge round stone. No amount of pushing, pulling or prodding managed to shift it. It had been cunningly engineered to seal the treasure room with everything inside it.

We were buried alive.

CHAPTER NINETEEN

The Howling of the Wolves

Back in the treasure room we sat on the ground, close to the lamp. The water and honey cake had revived Selene. She peered at me, then at Thrax. 'The child-men,' she whispered hoarsely.

'Let's have a bit of honey cake ourselves,' said Thrax. 'And a gulp of water. They'll help us think. But we must leave some food for later. We have no idea how long we're going to be in here.'

I chewed my cake in silence and took a large swig from the water flask. Thrax started rubbing his twisted ankle, trying very hard not to wince at the pain. He stared at the lamp and I knew once again he was working things out in his mind.

I had no idea how long we sat there, huddled together in the feeble light. I tried to concentrate on finding a way out of the tomb but the task seemed impossible. My mind is not as disciplined as Thrax's. It kept wandering back to the same question about Belos and Abantes.

Why did they want Selene dead?

I was sure Thrax had figured that out already but I couldn't interrupt him while he was thinking, and not with Selene listening.

Gradually, I became aware of a faint eerie sound, like a strong wind in the trees. But there was no wind in here, and no trees. I hoped it was not the moaning of the ancient king's ghost, wandering around its tomb looking for the stolen treasure.

'The sacred wolves,' whispered Selene, struggling to get the words out. 'They come in and out of the mountains.'

'Selene is right,' said Thrax, sitting up on one elbow. 'It is wolves howling.' He scrambled to his feet, wincing at the pain in his twisted ankle. 'If there's a way for wolves to get in here, there might be a way for us to get out. Or at least for one of us to go and fetch help.'

He spoke to Selene. 'Nico and I are going to look for the wolves before the oil in the alabastron runs out. We'll come back for you, I promise.'

He held the water bottle to her lips again and gave her the last of the honey cake. Then we both shinned back down the rope. The sound of wolves was definitely louder in the pit, and much clearer.

Thrax held the light close to the ground, swinging it in wide arcs. 'Hey, look, Nico.'

Peering in the light, I could make out a cluster of tiny dark blobs on the ground. 'Wolf poo,' I said.

Thrax nudged a lump gently with his toe. 'And it's fresh. The wolves were in here while we were in the chamber above. Let's find out where they're coming in. There must be a hole or a large crack somewhere.'

It was not easy finding the hole. The walls of the cave were patterned with dark shadows. To make matters worse, our light was guttering. I was thinking of adding a new strip of cloth from my chiton when I heard a soft, rustling sound behind me. A wolf-cub had her snout in my bag, which I had dropped on the floor.

She froze the moment I moved, her bushy tail held up stiff behind her. 'Thrax!' The wolf-cub pulled her head out of my bag and fixed me with small amber eyes. Her tail twitched and in a flash, she was gone.

'Did you see where she went?' said Thrax.

'Yes, she went round that rock in the corner.'

We rushed behind the rock and Thrax shone the light against the rough wall.

'Eureka! I've found it.'

The light had revealed a large hole about a knee's height off the ground. It was packed with loose stones that had a crack between them, wide enough for a wolf-cub to squeeze through. Thrax started pulling out the stones. I put the alabastron on the ground and joined him. A slight breeze touched my face as we dislodged more stones. Fresh air! On the other side of this wall, there was a connection with the outside world.

We soon had a pile of rubble on the floor and the hole was much deeper. 'There's a proper tunnel here,' said Thrax. 'It's just about wide enough for a person to crawl in. I think tomb robbers used it to get into the treasure chamber above us.'

His theory was proved right when we discovered a cracked skull in the debris. The tunnel must have collapsed with someone still inside it.

'Did the tomb robbers dig it themselves, do you think?' I asked, trying not to shudder as Thrax handed me the skull and I put it down gingerly on the ground.

'No, the walls are too smooth to have been made with human tools. I think it was carved by an underground river thousands of years ago. The tomb robbers were just lucky to find it.'

'As are we,' I said. Before long we had removed enough stones for Thrax to wriggle into the tunnel. He passed more stones back to me, which I added to the ever-growing pile.

The stones ran out halfway through the tunnel, the rest of which Thrax said was clear. 'Listen,' he called out in an echoey voice. 'Can you hear that?'

I stuck my head in and listened. 'It's the sound of water.'

'A river,' said Thrax. 'Rushing down the mountain. It might be a small tributary of the Pleistos, which starts on Mount Parnassus and flows all the way down to the Corinthian gulf.'

He wriggled on in the dark, dragging himself along on his elbows. Soon I could see the soles of his sandals coming back, dusty white in the darkness. He stood up, shaking grit out of his hair. His face glistened in the lamplight; it was covered in spray.

'The tunnel comes out more or less at my height above the riverbank,' he said breathlessly. 'The river's pretty fast. I guess its swollen by the recent rains. If we could find something to ride on, it'll take us out into the open at some point. Hand me the lamp, Nico, and follow me.'

He went back into the tunnel feet first. I followed, wriggling forwards on my tummy, praying I wouldn't get stuck. At the far end, we dropped out on to a narrow ledge, which was slippery underfoot. The sound of the river was deafening and, within moments, we were both soaked to the skin.

'If only we had a boat of some kind,' I shouted at Thrax, 'or at least a raft.'

'A raft,' Thrax shouted back. 'Good thinking, Nico. Let's see if we can find anything to build one.'

The gods were with us. We worked our way along the ledge till we came to a bend in the river. And there, trapped against the curved wall, was a small pile of thick branches. I had no idea how they'd got there but Thrax had an answer right away.

'I guess they were part of a raft,' he said. 'The tomb robbers must have had the same idea as us. They made a raft to get to the tunnel. Only they lost control it and came to grief against the rocks.'

'The robbers' tragedy is our good fortune,' I said.

We dragged the branches on to the ledge, struggling to keep a hold on the slippery bark. When we had them laid out side by side, I tore my himation into strips and helped Thrax lash the strongest ones together.

The raft built, we hurried back to the treasure room. Thrax used a sharp stone from the riverbank to smash Selene's chains. I had filled my flask at the river and we gave her more water. She got shakily to her feet.

'Lean on me, Selene,' said Thrax. 'We're getting you out of here.'

By the time we reached the riverbank, the lamp had gone out. Still, it was not completely dark. The river seemed to have its own light, a mysterious glow that made it possible for us to tread safely along the ledge.

We helped Selene aboard the raft, then Thrax and I pushed it into the water. We only had a moment to leap on board before the current caught us and whipped us away. At first the raft spun as if it were being sucked into Charybdis's jaws and I was sure we were all going to be thrown off. But once round the bend we stopped spinning. The current swept us along at great speed and we had to hold on to each other to stay on. Our faces were lashed with freezing water, which stung our faces and got into our eyes.

For most of the time, the roof of the watery tunnel was high above us but sometimes it swooped down so low we had to duck or we'd have smashed our heads against the rock.

Once we burst through a colony of bats hanging from the ceiling. They panicked and whirled around us, squeaking and flapping their pointed wings.

Selene, who had closed her eyes, opened them again. She lashed out with her arms in a panic.

'Harpies,' she screamed, hitting out at the creatures. 'Harpies. They're after us!'

The bats were left behind in an instant as the raft hurtled on. The branches bucked and jiggled underneath us, putting a terrific strain on the linen straps. I was sure most of them were going to snap any moment, hurling us into the roaring water.

'Hey, look,' said Thrax, nudging me in the ribs. 'I think there might be light up ahead.'

I became aware of a blurry glow in the distance. It grew larger and brighter, even as I looked. A few moments later, the raft shot out into blinding sunshine. My hands raked the air, trying to find something to hold on to. For a moment, I caught sight of the twin cliffs behind Delphi. Then I plummeted, screaming at the top of my lungs, and plunged into swirling water.

When I surfaced, Thrax was swimming towards a grassy bank with Selene in his arms. I caught up with him and we lifted her up on to the grass.

'Is she all right?' I said.

'She's unconscious. I think she's swallowed a lot of water.'

He nodded at the twin cliffs looming above us. 'We've landed somewhere outside Delphi. I think this pool must feed the famous Castalian spring. You go and fetch help, Nico. I'll stay and look after Selene.'

I started off towards Delphi, struggling to walk in my wet, torn chiton. It was late afternoon, almost sundown, and the city was humming with new pilgrims come to consult the oracle. Yet no one gave me a second look as I waddled up the hill towards Selene's farm and opened the gate.

Selene's mother was feeding the goats as I came down the path. Her eyes grew wide the moment she saw me and the bag of feed slipped out of her hands.

'Selene?' she cried. 'Have you found her? Is she alive?'

CHAPTER TWENTY

Thrax Explains

Glykon the magistrate reclined on a couch in his andron, picking nuts from a small dish decorated with silhouettes of robins in flight.

'Dear boys,' he said. 'Your master told me all about your adventure in Corinth on our trip to Kirrha. Have you been involved in another mystery, here in Delphi?'

'They certainly have, sir,' replied Master Ariston. 'It's astonishing what these two manage to get up to behind my back. Although I have to confess that this time I played a small but crucial part in the drama too…'

When Selene's parents had brought her home from the pool under the cliffs, we had rushed back to the country house. We found Master Ariston both worried and angry.

'You have been gone for nearly two days,' he wailed. 'I was starting to think you'd run away.'

We filled him in with all that had happened since Belos set the tree house on fire.

'These are serious crimes you accuse Abantes of,' he said when we finished. 'We must go and see Glykon the magistrate at once.'

So here we were, in Delphi's finest andron again, seated near the archon himself.

'I am afraid,' said Master Ariston, accepting a cup of wine from a slave, 'that the implications of this case are far-reaching, sir…'

'Let the boys tell me themselves,' said Glykon, sipping his wine as if he were about to enjoy an entertainment at a symposium.

'We have uncovered a crime, sir,' said Thrax. 'Possibly two, committed by the same person.'

The archon's eyes grew wide with interest and he leaned forward on his couch in anticipation. 'Tell me all.'

'As you know,' said Thrax, 'we are staying in a country house on the outskirts of Delphi while Master Ariston is writing a play.'

'It's called *The Dolphins*,' announced Master Ariston. 'It's based in holy Delphi itself. It starts with...'

The archon glared and raised an eyebrow at the interruption.

'We have our food and wine delivered every morning by a farmer's family who live nearby,' continued Thrax. 'The eldest daughter, Zoe, usually brings the supplies. There is a second girl, Selene, who is considered a bit strange and often gets into trouble with local kids who see her as a target for their pranks.

'One morning our food was not delivered as usual and when Nico and I went to collect it, we found the family very upset. It seemed Selene had run away after a furious argument with her father. The mother begged me to find the girl and bring her back. I couldn't turn down a grieving mother, so Nico and I agreed to take on the case.

'I soon deduced that Selene had not left of her own free will, as her father suspected. She had been kidnapped. There were some savings and a precious amulet hidden in Selene's room, which she would have taken with her if she'd run away.

'So now Nico and I were faced with three important questions. Who had kidnapped Selene? Why? And where was she being held?'

'And I should think there was a fourth question,' said the archon. 'Could you bring Selene back home?'

'Of that I had no doubt, sir,' replied Thrax. 'I was determined to bring her back. I myself come from a family that was torn apart and I understand the pain such separation causes.'

'But you had no guarantee that you could,' argued the archon. 'The girl could have been kidnapped by mountain bandits and dragged off into slavery.'

'I had a hunch that she was still on the mountain, sir,' said Thrax. 'And that was confirmed when some goatherds told us bandits haven't been able to use the mountain pass on Mount Parnassus for months. It has been blocked by a rockfall.'

'We do have occasional earth tremors in Delphi,' said the magistrate. 'I remember one last winter, in fact. Perhaps that caused the rockfall.'

'I had a strong feeling that the kidnapper was from Delphi,' continued Thrax. 'Nico and I made enquiries at the agora and we found out that Selene is a seer. She uses knucklebones to tell people's futures. Her mentor is a woman who has a similar gift, except she uses pebbles for her fortune telling. She works up in the Corcyian cave. People call her Mother Kessandra.

'We visited Mother Kessandra and learned that Selene had consulted her about a recurring nightmare she'd been having. A bad dream in which she is chased along a dark river by a man on a turtle.'

'Surely you did not base your investigations on a *dream*?' gasped Glykon.

'Some people believe that dreams are messages from the gods,' said Thrax. 'I think the messages come not from the gods but from somewhere deep inside our minds, to help us deal with things we are scared of. I believed Selene had actually met this man in real life and the hidden part of her mind was warning her that he was very dangerous.'

'But a man on a turtle is such a fanciful thing,' said the magistrate.

'As it turned out, Nico and I did meet a man on a turtle just outside Kirrha,' said Thrax. 'His name is Milo and he was on his way to Delphi with his father, who wanted to consult the oracle.

'There were things about Milo that made me suspicious at once. He had bruises on his face that had clearly been inflicted by some other man. And what man of his upbringing gets into fistfights? I became even more suspicious when he was introduced to Abantes, the priest at your symposium. The two pretended not to know each other. But I had seen Abantes and Milo together at the agora the day before. Abantes had his face hidden in a hood but there was no mistaking his limp, which later I learned was the result of a battle wound.

'That made Nico and I think that Milo might be the kidnapper. But that was not the case. Milo is involved in the mystery but he didn't kidnap Selene.

'And then I remembered that I had seen the man on the turtle in Delphi itself. Not a real person but a golden one. On a fibula, hidden under a boy's himation. This boy is called Belos. He's the baker's apprentice and he's a thug. He's made it one of his life's missions to bully Selene. I got into a scrap with him on our first night in Delphi and that's when I saw the fibula.

'During your symposium, Abantes mentioned that he'd bought a new fibula for his chlamys because he'd lost his old one, a pin his father had made using a symbol of Aegina, the island of turtles, but Abantes hadn't lost the pin. He'd given it to his son. Belos.'

The archon sat up, spilling wine on his couch. 'Abantes has a son?'

'He had to keep him a secret,' said Thrax, 'because when Belos was born in Delphi, Abantes's wife in Aegina was still alive. As you know, it is a crime to be unfaithful to your wife. The moment I realised there was a connection between Abantes and Belos, and that Milo was not the kidnapper, everything fell into place. I realised who had actually kidnapped Selene and why.'

'My dear boy, you have me in a spin,' said the archon, taking more wine and signalling a slave to hand out nuts to the rest of us. 'How can Milo be a victim and also be involved in committing a crime?'

Thrax continued. 'Milo's father is a merchant from New Sybaris called Gorgias. He came to Delphi seeking advice from the oracle about a precious ring he'd lost. This was no ordinary ring. It was a priceless piece of jewellery decorated with harpies. Gorgias's dying brother had made him promise that he'd give it to his long-lost daughter. The gods would put the curse of the harpies on Gorgias if he failed to give his niece the ring.

'Gorgias had lost the ring and he'd come to ask the oracle where he might find it. Two days ago,

Nico and I trailed Milo to a disused farm outside Kirrha where he had a secret meeting. The men he met were part of a gang. He owed them money. That's when I realised Gorgias hadn't lost the ring. His son Milo had stolen it to pay off some of his gambling debts. He was desperate to stop his father from finding out about it. So he had come to Delphi to make sure the oracle did not reveal his guilty secret.'

The magistrate's put down his cup down. 'How could he do that?'

'It is my understanding,' said Thrax, 'that when the Pythia is possessed by the god, she speaks in his mysterious language. She herself does not understand it. Only trained priests like Abantes know what the words mean and they write them down on a tablet, which they give to the pilgrim. I believe Milo came to Delphi to bribe the Pythia's priest to lie about the ring, to write down something other than the truth. It was a desperate plan made by a desperate person but he got lucky. Abantes accepted the bribe.'

'My boy,' gasped the magistrate, 'are you aware of what you are saying? Accepting bribes to twist the Pythia's message is a serious crime. If word got out that the oracle is corrupt, that it is not the absolute word of Apollo, it would ruin Delphi, and perhaps oracles all over the Hellenic world.'

'The crime didn't happen,' said Thrax. 'Because something went wrong with the plan. On the day Gorgias was expecting to consult the Pythia, an important general from Sparta arrived and Gorgias lost his place in the queue. Milo and Abantes were not expecting this. They were forced to postpone their plan for another month.

'And then another complication arose. While Milo and Abantes were talking about their plan, someone overheard them. Selene. Abantes had no choice but to get rid of her before she told anyone what she'd heard.'

The archon rose to his feet. 'These are very serious accusations, young man. But there is only one way to find out the truth. We must speak to Selene herself.'

CHAPTER TWENTY ONE

Messages from the Knucklebones

We all hurried to Selene's house right away. She was sitting up in Zoe's bed, her mum insisting she eat some hot stew.

She confirmed that Thrax was right. After her visit to Mother Kessandra in the winter, she had spotted Abantes during one of her secret trips to the agora. She had noticed his turtle fibula and wondered if he was the man in her nightmare.

From then on she started shadowing him at every opportunity, hoping to discover more about him. Two days before Gorgias tried to consult the oracle, she had eavesdropped on Abantes and Milo discussing their dastardly plan in the agora. She thought no one would notice her hiding place in a nearby doorway. But she was wrong. Abantes had spotted her. And he had persuaded Belos to help him kidnap her. Belos had told her as much when she was chained to the wall in the king's treasure chamber.

The magistrate listened closely to Selene's story. When she finished, he got to his feet and sent a city guard to arrest Belos and Abantes. 'My dear young woman,' he said, 'Delphi owes you a big apology. But it is very important that news of this debacle stays within these four walls. I have been told that you are a seer yourself. Delphi has had old Pythias for many years now. Perhaps we should go back to the ancient times and have a young priestess to speak the words of Apollo. How would you like to be the oracle's new Pythia?'

Selene accepted at once and her mother also took the opportunity to try and pay Thrax, which he refused.

'I agree with the young man,' said the archon. 'Keep your hard-earned money, woman. The city of Delphi will reward these two young men for their bravery... and their loyal silence.'

* * *

Selene spent the next two days preparing for her new life as the Pythia. Zoe came to see us on the sixth day of the month. She brought an invitation from Selene. Would Thrax and I like to watch her first communication with the god?

The ceremony to consult the oracle was long and full of ritual. The Pythia, attended by the priests of the oracle, purified herself in the Castalian spring, then lead a small crowd of attendants and temple officials along the Sacred Way to the sanctuary.

Here, at an altar, a young goat was sprinkled with salt and sacred water. It trembled, a sign that the god was present. The animal was sacrificed, the smoke from the altar a sign that the oracle would speak.

Then Selene entered the temple, where a light burned at a smaller altar dedicated to Hestia. Here the pilgrims, including Thrax and myself, offered a honey cake, a token of our gratitude to the oracle. Selene retreated to a restricted chamber at the back of the temple, the adyton, where only priests and priestesses are allowed. She removed her veil. In the light of Hestia's fire, she did not look like a child any more, but a messenger of the gods, full of their power. People say that the Pythia is the most powerful woman in the Hellenic world. Looking at Selene now, I knew she was also going to be one of the most respected.

Selene took her place on a three-legged stool and gazed into a dish full of water from the sacred spring. Close to her was the round stone known as the omphalos. It was guarded by two enormous statues of eagles, both covered in gold.

The temple filled with smoke, almost hiding Selene and her attendants from view. It became difficult to breathe, and my eyes stung. Selene started rocking back and forth on her stool. A long, keening sound came out of her mouth.

A priest brought in the first pilgrim. Gorgias.

'Do you seek the wisdom of sacred Apollo?' asked the priest.

'I do.'

'Then ask your question.'

'I seek a precious ring that was lost. Where should I look for it?'

Selene closed her eyes. Her moaning turned to wailing and she writhed like the wounded Python, the dragon whose name she had inherited.

Suddenly she opened her eyes wide and I was shocked to see they had turned purple. She spat out a string of wild, scary-sounding words. Then she slumped forward and two attendants rushed to save her from crashing to the ground.

The priest, a replacement for Abantes, wrote down her message on a wax tablet, which he handed to Gorgias. The merchant did not look at it but held it close to his chest. He bowed to the Pythia and left the temple. We left with him.

*   *   *

Selene's father invited us to a meal at his farm that night, to celebrate Selene becoming the Pythia, and to thank us for rescuing her. We ate in the kitchen but afterwards Selene asked us to join her in the shed. She wasn't sleeping in it any more. As the Pythia, she now lived in a grand house in the centre of Delphi. But – she explained – she would keep coming here when she wanted to be on her own, away from the pressures of her new position.

'I will now read the knucklebones for you,' she said, as we all squeezed into the small room. She pulled a small bag from her chiton. 'It will be my payment to you for saving my life.' She opened the bag and let the knucklebones cascade on to the floor. 'You throw first, Nico.'

I gathered the knucklebones and scattered them again. Selene looked over them carefully, moving a finger from one bone to the other.

'You have a bright future ahead of you, Nico. People will enjoy your stories. They will bring you fame and fortune. But do not be disheartened if at first you do not find favour with the public. Your gift will be recognised in due course.'

She scooped up the knucklebones and dropped them in Thrax's hands. 'Now it's your turn.'

Thrax blew on them as if he were throwing dice at a game and let them fall to the floor. 'May luck be with me.'

Selene brought a lamp closer. 'You seek someone you lost a long time ago,' she said. 'Someone you still love very much. She is out there, waiting for you, for her heart tells her that you are still alive. But your quest will bring great and terrible danger, both for you and the woman you seek. May Apollo and Gaia, the ancient earth goddess, protect you both...'

CHAPTER TWENTY TWO

A New Adventure

The day after the oracle had spoken, Zoe helped Thrax and I clean the country house. Once it was spotless, we packed our belongings. Master Ariston had received great news and was eager to leave Delphi. He had been invited to stage his first play – at Corinth.

'It's not even finished yet,' he crowed, holding tight his small statue of Apollo, 'and I am already a great success. The oracle was right.'

Thrax and I were overjoyed to be going to Corinth too. We would meet up with the other members of our secret society, Fotini and Gaia. We had a lot to tell them about our adventure in Delphi, and perhaps we would solve another mystery with them there.

After supper, we went to say goodbye to Selene and her family. Selene's mother gave us some sausages for the journey. 'But make sure you have some yourselves,' she said. 'Don't let your master eat them all.'

Zoe, who'd been delivering honey cakes around Delphi, had lots of news. The city guards had found Belos hiding in the cellar under the bakery. He'd been thrown in prison.

No one knew where Abantes was. Some said he'd been spotted in the harbour, bribing a sea captain to take him back to Aegina. Others insisted that goatherds had seen him on a mountain pass, a heavy sack on his back.

'Can we speak to you alone?' Thrax asked Selene.

Selene showed us to her shed, where we all squeezed inside again.

'Nico and I have a secret society,' said Thrax at once. 'It has four members so far. Nico, myself and two girls from Corinth. They helped us solve our first case last year. We would like you to become the fifth member.'

'What does your secret society do?' asked Selene.

'We fight crime wherever we find it,' I said.

'That's a very noble cause,' said Selene. 'I would be honoured to join.'

Thrax smiled and pulled a small charm of the Medusa from his chiton. We had bought it at the agora that morning and it looked very much like the ones we had round our necks.

'Our society is called the Medusa League. This is our secret badge.'

Selene slipped the charm over her neck. 'I shall wear it proudly and I shall answer your call for help when it comes. Perhaps I will need your help one day too, in which case I'll send a messenger.'

Thrax and I said our goodbyes before hurrying back to the city. There was just enough time to have one last look around before we left.

'Hey, Nico,' said Thrax. 'Do you realise we've never been to visit the stadium up in the hills? Come on, let's go and have a look at it now. We may never come to Delphi again.'

We hurried along the Sacred Way and up to the stadium, which was nestled under a cliff. It was deserted and the moonlight shone on the empty stone seats.

'I wish we'd been here for the Pythian Games,' said Thrax wistfully.

'Yes,' I said, 'that would have been amazing. They have a music festival too, although how music carries in such a vast place I'll never know.'

'These places are specially built to carry sound,' said Thrax.

We spent some time exploring the place. Thrax pretended to wrestle with an invisible opponent. I sat on the stone seats, clapping and cheering him on.

'Isn't he the best?' I asked invisible spectators sitting on the seats on either side of me. 'Isn't he a champ?'

Thrax bowed his head to receive an imaginary crown, which he tossed up in the air. 'Come on, Nico. Race you to the gate. Master Ariston will be wondering where we are.'

We pelted up the steps towards the exit, Thrax running deliberately slowly to let me win. I was almost at the top when I bumped into a tall figure wrapped from head to toe in black. Thrax and I both stopped dead in our tracks as the figure revealed its face.

It was Abantes.

His eyes were little pools of anger, shining like burning coals in the falling dark. 'You think you have destroyed me,' he hissed. 'I have lost my position at the temple, my fortune will be taken from me and I will end up in prison if I'm caught. But I am not finished yet. By the breath of Cronus and the gods of darkness, I shall have my revenge on you two and the new Pythia. And I shall rise again, to everlasting fame and fortune.'

There was movement in the shadows behind him and a second figure slunk out from the trees.

Belos! He too was wearing black.

'Are you wondering how I managed to get out of prison?' he laughed. 'Well, I have a powerful father, with many connections still.'

Without warning, he leaped on Thrax and a knife flashed in his hands. I looked on, helpless, as they tumbled to the ground and Abantes roared with angry laughter.

'Oh, gods help us,' I cried. 'I beg you.'

The gods must have heard because, in a flash, I remembered something I had packed for the journey to Corinth. I opened my pouch and plunged my hand in.

'Belos,' I called, 'look over here!' And I hurled the contents of my ink bag straight in his face. He screamed as the ground charcoal blinded him and filled his mouth.

Thrax leaped to his feet. 'Thank you, Nico.'

'Thank the gods,' I said. 'They gave me the idea.'

We both tore down the hill, leaving Abantes to help a spluttering Belos. Coming closer to the city, we saw flaming torches bobbing in our direction. 'Whoa...' called a voice. 'Are you Nico the scribe and Thrax, Ariston the poet's slave?'

'We are,' called back Thrax. 'But Master Ariston is a playwright now, not a poet.'

'We are city guards,' said one of the men. 'The magistrate sent us to fetch you and someone said they saw you heading to the stadium. Master Glykon would like to see you before you leave.'

'City guards? What luck. We've just had a run-in with Abantes and his son!' said Thrax. 'You need to go after them at once.'

The city guard looked startled and peered around him. 'Abantes? Where?'

'On the steps to the stadium,' I said.

The guard dispatched some of the men to catch up with Abantes while he took us to the archon's house. Glykon was waiting for us with a gift. A leather purse packed tight with silver.

'This is payment from the oracle,' he said. 'Thank you once again for saving it from ridicule. But I beg you, not a word of this escapade to anyone.'

'I promise, not a word to anyone,' said Thrax.

I did not repeat what he said because I knew what I was going to do the moment I got home. I was going to start writing all about our adventure in Delphi. I had no worries about it. After all, Delphi had not been ruined. People who would read or listen to my story would take it as proof that the gods always protect their oracles.

'Ha,' I said to Thrax as we headed back to Master Ariston. That silver brings you another step closer to freedom.'

He looked at me with fierceness in his eyes. 'But I insist on sharing the reward.'

'I will not take an obol from you until you are a freeman like me,' I said. Thrax scowled. 'At least let me buy you a new tablet.'

* * *

The following day, at dawn, Nico saddled Ariana and we joined the stream of pilgrims flowing out of Delphi. We were starting on the road down to

Kirrha when Gorgias caught up with us. Milo was with him, his face hidden deep inside his himation.

'I want to thank you,' he said to Thrax, 'for bringing my son's gambling debts to my attention. I shall pay them off as soon as we return to New Sybaris. My son feared I would cut him out of my will if I found out he was a gambler. I shall do no such thing, of course. I will stand by him. He is a good son, despite his failings.'

'And you are a good father. The gods bless you,' said Master Ariston.

Gorgias grinned for ear to ear. It was the first time I'd seen him look happy.

'And have you heard the news?' he said. 'The city guards arrested the priest Abantes and a boy called Belos for trying to kidnap Selene the goatherd and sell her to mountain bandits. The pair managed to give them the slip, though. The gods only know where the rascals are hiding now.'

'But what about the oracle, Gorgias?' asked Master Ariston. 'What advice did she give you about the ring of the harpies?'

'You will hardly believe it,' said the merchant. 'I might be a long way from evading the curse of the harpies, but the Pythia's words fill me with hope.'

He held up the wax table to show us what the priest in the temple had written on it:

To find the lost treasure and lift the curse of the harpies, the merchant must enlist the help of a scribe and a slave.

'Well, I never,' gasped Master Ariston.

Thrax and I looked at each other with wide grins on our faces. It seemed our next adventure had begun already.

Bonus Bits!

Greek gods and myths

Thrax and Nico, the main characters in our story, lived in a period of Greek history known today as Classical Greece. It lasted from around 510 to 323BC. The age when myth and history merged was long gone. People still believed in the ancient gods, though. They prayed and sacrificed to them often and referred to them all the time. Here is a list of the gods and some mythical creatures mentioned in our story.

Aphrodite goddess of love and beauty. Her special symbol was the evening star. She was also associated with the sea and often depicted in art swimming with dolphins and swans, or surrounded by pearls.

Aphaia   goddess who was only worshipped on the island of Aegina. She had a famous temple there. Pregnant mothers prayed to her. She was also associated with the changing seasons. In time, people from outside the island started calling her Athena Aphaia

Apollo   god of music and poetry. A beautiful young man, his symbol was the lyre. When only four days old, Apollo was believed to have killed a serpent-like dragon called the Python.

Aristaios   god of many food-making crafts, including the making of cheese, olive oil, herbal medicines and honey. He also protected beekeepers and shepherds.

Artemis   goddess of hunting, wild animals and untamed places. Her symbols were the bow, the arrow, hunting dogs, the moon and – most famously – the stag. People in the ancient world believed she drove a chariot drawn by deer. Her sacred animals included the bear but also small birds like partridges and quails.

Athena goddess of many things, including wisdom, mathematics, war and heroes. Her many symbols included the owl, the olive tree, the shield, the spear and a protective amulet with the Medusa's face on it.

Cronus god of time and king of the Titans. He was the father of Zeus and also ruled over the Elysian Islands, the home of the blessed dead. His name actually means 'time'. People were scared of him because they knew that time destroyed everything.

Dionysus god of wine, the grape harvest, merrymaking and theatre. Many illustrations of him show him as a well-rounded old man but he is sometimes drawn as a younger person too. He was looked after by magical rain nymphs when he was a child.

Gaia mother of all creation. She was born at the dawn of time. On Greek vases, she was always drawn as a chubby woman full of life and health. In mosaics, she was often shown wearing green, a symbol of growth.

Gorgons monstrous women with snakes for hair. If you looked at a gorgon you would turn to stone. Medusa is now the most famous of the gorgons.

Harpies horrible birds with the faces of ugly women. In a famous legend, they tortured King Phineus by continually snatching his food and pooing on the scraps left behind. Jason and the Argonauts saved him by chasing away the harpies.

Hera the mother goddess. She was married to Zeus, the chief god and was the protector of women, marriage and family. Believed to be a very serious person, she was often depicted on a throne. The peacock, the cow and the lily were some of her many symbols.

Hermes god of thieves, travellers and athletes. Believed to be quick on his feet and able to slip easily from the mortal world into the mystical one, he acted as a messenger for the other gods. He was also honoured as the god of boundaries between countries and worlds.

Hestia goddess of the hearth, the family and the home. She was Zeus's sister. She is usually depicted with a staff or by a large fire.

Medusa a gorgon, a monster with snakes for hair. If anyone looked into her eyes, they were turned immediately to stone. Medusa had two sisters who were immortal. They could not be killed. The hero Perseus managed to cut off Medusa's head. He escaped being turned to stone by only looking at the gorgon's reflection in his shield.

Pan god of shepherds and hunters. He also protected the forests and the meadows. In art, he was always shown as a man with the horns, tails and legs of a goat. He also had a very thick beard and pointy ears. Pan played the pipes, always hidden from the view of mortals. He liked chasing nymphs.

Poseidon   god of the sea. He was also known as the earth-shaker because he was able to cause earthquakes. He could create islands and springs by striking rocks with his trident. Sailors prayed to him for protection while fishermen left their tridents in his temple when they retired.

Zeus   the chief god on Mount Olympus, he ruled over the other gods with a fiery temper. All the other gods rose to their feet when he was present. His special symbols were the oak, the bull and the thunderbolt, which he loved hurling at his enemies.

GLOSSARY

Thrax and Nico use many Greek words in their second adventure. Here is a list of what they mean.

Adyton   a restricted part of a temple that only priests can enter

Agora   a marketplace, also used for public meetings

Alabastron   a perfume jar, sometimes worn around the neck

Andron   a special room where men relaxed and held parties

Aulos   a musical instrument made with two reed pipes

Chiton   a long tunic, often made of wool

Epiblema   a warm shawl, usually worn in cold weather

Fibula   a brooch or a clasp

Himation   a long woollen garment worn over the left shoulder

Hoplites   Greek citizens who also acted as soldiers

Hydria   wide pot used for carrying water

Khaire   ancient Greek word which meant 'rejoice'. It was used like our 'hello'

Kylix   a two-handled drinking cup

Obol   a coin

Omphalos   a stone said to represent the belly button of the world

Peplos a long robe, worn by women

Petasos a sun hat

Pythia the priestess of the oracle at Delphi

Thugater ancient Greek for 'daughter'

Tiganites wheat pancakes, usually eaten for breakfast